Bon's Echo

Patricia Runyon

iUniverse, Inc.
Bloomington

Bon's Echo

iUniverse books may be ordered through booksellers or by contacting:

iUniverse
1663 Liberty Drive
Bloomington, IN 47403
www.iuniverse.com
1-800-Authors (1-800-288-4677)

Because of the dynamic nature of the Internet, any web addresses or links contained in this book may have changed since publication and may no longer be valid. The views expressed in this work are solely those of the author and do not necessarily reflect the views of the publisher, and the publisher hereby disclaims any responsibility for them.

Any people depicted in stock imagery provided by Thinkstock are models, and such images are being used for illustrative purposes only.
Certain stock imagery © Thinkstock.

ISBN: 978-1-4759-2411-4 (sc)
ISBN: 978-1-4759-2413-8 (hc)
ISBN: 978-1-4759-2412-1 (ebk)

Printed in the United States of America

iUniverse rev. date: 05/10/2012

Oh, how I longed to roam. I dreamed of adventures, reckless meetings with destiny, but like most kids, I was smarter than that. Sometimes the best journeys you'll go on are when your mind goes and your feet stay. No dangerous people, lost luggage, or lack of funds.

For my daddy.

Chapter 1

"Chris!" A female voice cut through the stillness.

I was ripped from a comatose sleep in a panic. It wasn't a fire or family brawl—it was worse. It was Wednesday, and I had to get ready for school. I allowed my pulse to return to normal while I lay there and wondered about my mother. Can you believe that woman used to sing me awake?

"I'm up!" I called as loud as my sleepy vocal cords would permit. I pulled off my torn blankets and readied myself for a more vertical pose, but every muscle failed me. I just lay there. I kept my eyes closed, refusing to let reality in.

My mother was chemically depressed, among other things. A psychiatric oddity who smoked cheap ultra-light cigarettes, she was just your average barrel of dysfunctional monkeys all on her own. I could've elaborated on that subject at some length, but I was anticipating the inevitable.

"Chris!"

Ah, there it was.

"Yeah, okay, I'm getting there," I said, pushing my legs off the bed to rest my feet on the floor. My name wasn't really Chris, it was Christy, but you couldn't tell I was a girl by looking at me. To my shame I was going through puberty. I hid it desperately by dressing like a boy, hence everyone called me Chris. The other girls my age were, in my opinion, excessively excited about developing boobs. I thought mammary glands were overrated and a stupid thing to obsess over. They would be practical, but I didn't understand the intrigue.

I picked out an outfit that left all flesh to the imagination and stumbled into the hall.

"See, I'm up," I said to my mother in the kitchen before entering the yellow cubical bathroom. I closed the door, and to my horror found myself looking right back in the mirror. "God, I wish I hadn't gotten all the shitty recessive genes." I turned my back to the mirror and began to brush my teeth.

I lived in Canon City, Colorado, a growing town of drunks and Holy Rollers. The majority of the population was incarcerated in the neighboring correctional facilities.

I rinsed my toothbrush and then washed my face. There was a sudden drumming on the door.

"What?" I yelled, quickly getting dressed.

"Get out! I gotta pee!" my older brother David whined from the hall.

David was seventeen and took after my father, with dark hair and eyes, a little short but good-looking. He had a new girlfriend at least every three months, and my mother was always giving him safe-sex lectures. My brother was a genius. I knew this because everyone told me about it and then, in soft, concerned voices, asked me how I was doing in school. I had to tell them that I thought I was passing, maybe. David was a cocky jerk, and for the most part, I didn't like him. Was I jealous? Probably.

When I opened the door, David rushed in, threw me out, and slammed the door.

"Christ!" I exclaimed as I struggled to find my balance. "What a freak!" I stood there for a moment, kicked the door, and moved into the bedroom I shared with both my siblings.

Brittany was still sleeping soundly when I entered. I loudly shoved my school books into my black backpack and fought with

2

the broken zipper. Brittany was seven and took after my mother, with delicate blond curls, baby-blue eyes, pale skin, and soft features. She looked like a porcelain doll and acted accordingly, as if she were in a Hollywood horror movie. She was more manipulative than a big-breasted gold digger. Did I mention she was also a genius? I must have been left on the doorstep as a baby.

"Get up!" I said, pulling her blanket off.

She just growled and pulled it back up over her head. "Leave me alone, transvestite!"

I laughed, shrugging off her hearsay insult, but knowing it wasn't far from the truth. I wasn't a lesbian; I just hated myself, although my parents' suspicion concerning my sexual preference had saved me from being included in safe-sex lectures. I had short, medium-brown hair, eyes that wouldn't pick a color, and I weighed more than I should. I wasn't naturally disposed to getting the grade. I had to work to get that C-plus, and at the ripe age of thirteen, I had no hope of achieving prom queen.

Aside from my overly publicized faults (thank you, family), I did have some things they didn't. I could write. My world in ink set me apart from the rest of my family, and I prided myself on that. I could draw and paint too. What I lacked in social expectation I made up for with creativity.

I walked into the living room and sat on the outdated, brown couch next to my dad. The morning news was on the box in front of us. Through the hollow cheer of the TV anchors, my father asked, "Did you get your homework done?" in his demeaning manner designed just for me.

"Yeah," I replied, half lying.

"Dan, don't forget to take out the trash again!" my mother's disembodied voice hollered from somewhere in the house.

"I told you already that I will get it when I leave for work!" my dad yelled back impatiently.

My parents fought constantly. They would pick at each other, explode, and break the furniture. I often listened in amazement. *That's what it'll be like to be grown up?* I thought. I rehearsed with my stuffed bear for the retarded arguments I'd save for when I was grown. In the meantime, I'd amuse myself by accusing Mr. Bear of leaving the toilet seat up. I always felt like I should break something just to get the full experience of it all.

Looking at the clock, I decided to leave for school a half hour early. I stood up, threw my bag over my shoulder, and headed for the front door.

"You're not eating breakfast?" inquired my father.

"I'm not hungry."

"Going on a diet?" he said with a sincere and hopeful smile.

"No," I whispered and slipped out the door. *Unconditional love plays no part in my screwed-up family,* I thought as the wish to self-destruct took over. I got enough shit for being fat at school; I didn't need it from my family too.

I walked the downtown alleyways, hiding from the street sweeper and the cars of the working dead. I tried to convince myself I could be invisible as a virus, a game I continued until I was sure I'd be late for class.

"Bon, are you even listening to me?" called a loud, stern voice.

"What?" I yelled, violently yanked from a deep sleep, unaware of where I was or what I was doing there.

"I asked if you were listening."

"Yeah, every word." It was my shrink, and I was in her creepy office with floral-printed wallpaper.

"You've run away from home three times in the past two years," she said, as though it were news to me.

"So?" I rolled my eyes.

"Why would a smart boy like you be so stupid? You have a wonderful family and a promising future."

"Because it's what all the cool kids were doing at the time. Now they're stealing cars," I said trying to sound as confused as possible. "I just want people to like me."

She sighed and sat back in her chair. I was proud. She would get fed up with my bullshit and refuse to see me, just like the other shrink. Victory was mine. I didn't need help. It wasn't me; it was my fucking family.

I stared at the ceiling, trying my best to keep my eyes from drooping. I could see her intent, frustrated gaze from the corner of my eye. I felt a halfhearted pity for her; she was older than her age and was rushing for her grave. Premature wrinkles and early gray veiled her otherwise average appearance.

"You are wasting both of our time. Get serious or leave," she announced as she stood up. There were still thirty minutes before the session was supposed to be over. I stood up from the pink couch I was trying to fall asleep on.

"I'll just leave." I hated the whole building. It was three stories of nothing but shrinks and a lobby. I was dumbfounded and relieved at the fact I got to leave a half hour early. I smiled and walked out the door.

I wasn't really trying to gain popularity by running away. It was simple. My family was boring, and I didn't belong. I dreamed of more than what my family deemed "practical." My father was part of the hardworking middle class. My stepmother was a Martha Stewart wannabe, and my stepbrothers were high school football stars. I truly believed I had somehow become trapped in a sixties family sitcom—"Honey, I'm home." It creeped me out.

I walked through the lobby and out the front doors to behold the ninety-seven-degree city of Phoenix in springtime. Not a tough decision. I wasn't going to wait for my stepmother to pick me up. My parents had already decided that there was something "deeply troubling me." It was their conclusion that was my scapegoat. I could do what they expected me to do, even though my conscience may not agree. I was only a bad kid because they thought I was. How convenient for me. I headed to the nearest bus station and headed downtown.

Tears of frustration and disappointment soaked the sleeves of my red flannel jacket. With my elbows resting on the picnic table, I cradled my head and repeated rhythmically with my rocking, "Stupid, stupid, stupid."

I had failed my history test, and I had to get it signed by my parents. I just knew they would kill me. They would tell me what a piece of shit I was and how they wished I was never born. They compared me to David and Brittany too much. Those two were born smart. It's not fair. Why wasn't I a genius too? This was forever my quarrel with my creator.

You would have to have been in my shoes to understand the morbid justification of my self-loathing. My parents told me I should feel bad about being stupid, fat, and ugly, so I did. I felt like I did them honor by hating myself for the reasons they hated me.

At the park a block from my house, I sat indulging in the bitter tears of realization. *They're right about me.*

At the sound of footsteps, I looked up to see David approaching. "Mom made me come get you. We're eating dinner," he said. Realizing I had been crying, he rolled his eyes and walked back to the house.

I knew that I would be grounded as soon as I got home and showed my parents my test. I couldn't see a single good reason why I shouldn't beat the shit out of David right now. I wanted him to care, to be a big brother, but he just walked away. With each step he took, I could feel my anger boil, swell, and then explode with a burst of adrenalin. I sprinted after him, and with heavy momentum tackled him to the asphalt street. I let my anger consume me as I punched at his kidneys. Stunned and very pissed off, David tried using his wrestling techniques, but he was no match for a ballistic, self-destructive adolescent. My mouth was full of blood, but I couldn't feel a thing.

The time passed quickly, and before I knew it, the neighbors were pulling us apart. I could hear my father coming down the street.

"Hey, what the hell is going on?"

David, like the little bitch he was, ran to our dad to tell on me. I just lay down in the street, staring up at the faint, new stars. I felt a hell of a lot better—peaceful even.

After the neighbors left, my father pulled me home by my hair. My mother immediately took care of David's pretty face and the bite marks I'd left. I didn't remember biting him, but then I couldn't remember most of what happened. My dad spanked me with his bull leather belt. Not a normal custom, but one reserved for major fuck-ups. As my father coiled the belt, I couldn't stop myself from letting out a slight giggle.

"What the hell are you laughing about?" my father demanded.

"You don't even know the half of it." I started laughing, trying again to catch my decorum. "I failed my history test too! God, am I an asshole!" I couldn't stop laughing; I'd lost my entire grip on reality. I was a total loser and a waste of billions of years of evolution. The irony of my existence was hilarious.

After my beating, my parents started in with the really damaging things. Honestly, I would rather be beaten to the point of hospitalization than be told by my parents that they didn't love me.

I had spent my free afternoon and stolen evening reading graffiti and watching the crazies. As I relaxed in the park under a tree, my thoughts drifted. The cool evening air held me, and I couldn't help but to give in to the melancholy rhythm. It was time to run; I could feel it. I knew I couldn't stay if I wanted to. I had stagnated for the last nine months, my behavior had become more defiant, and the boredom was getting harder to ignore. I had been trying since the last time I was brought in, trying to make myself fit into my family, but it seemed that the harder I tried, the more in vain it felt. It was decided. Friday night, after everyone went to bed, I would sneak out my window and catch the eleven-thirty freight train. I lay under the tree for a while longer, planning, dreaming, and fearing the worst.

I got home around ten. To say the least, my father wasn't pleased with my absence.

"Where have you been?" he asked the second I opened the door.

"I was downtown at the park," I answered, trying to think of a decent excuse.

"We were worried about you. I called the hospital and had the police looking for you. You're only fourteen!" my dad said on the verge of crying. He threw his arms around me. "Would you please stop doing this to me?"

"I'm sorry. I just had a lot to think about."

"I don't care. You should've called or something!" He turned and went to the kitchen for an antacid.

"Look, I know I've been very inconsiderate, but I don't mean to be. I'm just depressed and confused," I said quoting my shrink. "But I want things to get better." My father, looking skeptical, returned to the living room where I stood. "I mean it. I want to try," I said, refusing to believe that they were my own words.

He smiled and gave me a warm hug that lasted for several moments. He stepped back and asked, "Does this mean you'll start talking with your psychiatrist?"

I had hoped it wouldn't come to that. "Yeah," I replied, trying my best to hide my disdain. I suppose I could talk to keep the peace. I only had two days to go and one appointment with her. How much damage could a shrink do?

We stayed up a while longer talking. I told him what he wanted to hear, and I was in bed by two. I must admit, I really loved that man—not for what he did, but for his intentions. He only wanted me to be well-adjusted and as happy as normality permits. I often wished he understood me, but I might as well have asked for snow in the summer. We were far too different. If we weren't family, I'm sure we wouldn't know each other at all. I sometimes wondered if my mother would've understood me. I had her brown eyes and dark hair. I wasn't even sure I shared genetics with my dad at all. He was only five-foot-seven with light brown hair, sharp features, and green-blue eyes. When I thought of my father, I thought of a heart of gold that had been just a little misguided, but whose wasn't?

I didn't go to public school, having missed too many days this year. My father thought it best I "catch up" in home school, not that I needed to. I had learned more riding the rails and talking to strangers than any censored textbook could have taught me. When I woke up, I did my chore for mediocrity as quickly as possible so that the rest of the day I could make my preparations. I discreetly wrote a list of supplies:

Lightweight blanket
Extra set of clothes
Space blankets
Journal
Travel sewing kit
Five-hour emergency candles
Toothbrush and paste
Bar of soap
Sterno
Sterno stove
MREs
Water jug
Lighters
Pens
First aid kit
Baby wipes
Birth certificate
Social security card
Money

That last one would be tricky. I had about fifty dollars saved in my dresser drawer, but I would need all I could get my hands on. Though it would cause a dilemma of conscience, I would have to steal from my dad. I imagined I'd take my stepbrothers' birthday money too, but I didn't feel bad about that. Knowing their mother would replace it as soon as the alarm was raised, I couldn't care less. They were spoiled. I always regretted taking from my dad; it was my only attack of emotion when planning my escape.

"Bon?" my stepmother said, opening my bedroom door. I frantically hid the list under my pillow. "What were you doing?" she asked, looking toward the pillow.

"Hum." I couldn't think of anything. There was a long, awkward silence, and then a look of relief washed over her face as she drew closer.

"It's perfectly normal for a boy your age to become interested in girls and the female body."

I was puzzled. What was she talking about? Then it dawned on me—she must have thought I was looking at one of my brother's T&A magazines. I could only giggle nervously.

"It's a natural curiosity. You don't have to be ashamed." She smiled, and I couldn't help but smile back. By smiling at her, she accepted her assumption as fact. "Just make sure you return it before they get home," she said as she backed from the room. "I won't tell them you borrowed it."

"Thanks," I said smiling, not able to believe what had just transpired.

"Oh, I almost forgot—I'm meeting your father for lunch. Did you want to come?"

"Nah, I think I might take a nap," I said. She nodded and smirked as if to say, "Yeah, right." She was implying that I wanted more time with the magazine I had in theory borrowed. Well, I guess that was better than finding out that I was going to run again. But geez, that's gross. With I.Q.s like my stepbrothers had, you could be quite sure they weren't reading the articles. If I were to borrow one of their girl mags, I might as well borrow underwear too. My stepmother left the room, but it took me a while to shake off the embarrassing experience and focus again. My stepmother left to meet my father, and I went to work gathering the supplies.

I had a large army back pack with several pockets in which I organized everything. There were still a few items I needed to get, but I figured I could just sneak out later and pick them up. I hid my backpack under my bed and anticipated the boredom of waiting.

Embarrassed by the wounds I had received while brawling with David, I skipped school the next day and spent the morning wondering around the Hog Back hills behind my house. My eyes searched the vast expanse of rolling, ancient seabed. Wouldn't it be wonderfully strange to run into a lost tragedy like myself out here hiding from the world as I was doing? I was sure I was this town's only mistake. I'd never be anything but lonely. My thoughts persisted, though I tried to turn off my mind. I walked for a couple hours, climbed to the tallest peak, and thought, *If I jumped, I think I could fly.* Instead, I spread my jacket over the dirt and lay down. Staring up into the blue sky, I let myself fall apart. My family couldn't love me, and I was tired of trying to love myself. My salted tears burned my bruised and cut face, and with each tear that stung, I shed twice as many. I couldn't go to school, not today or ever again. I was sick of it; I didn't want to share in this great miracle called life. If I were dead, I wouldn't be such a disappointment. I cried uncontrollably, and the tears felt like acid streaming down the sides of my face. The drops fell and soaked my red flannel jacket. Trapped in a personal hell, I couldn't see any other way out of being me. I reached into the right pocket of my jeans and recovered the new razor blade. Peeling off the protective paper covering, I wondered how long it would take for them to find my body. Wild animals

11

picking over my corpse wouldn't be much of an improvement to my looks, I supposed. I took a deep, calm breath. Then, with all the suppressed anger of thirteen years, I let myself scream and sent the razor swimming into my wrist. I closed my eyes, dropped my arms to my sides, and waited.

Chapter 2

My father had already called my shrink to inform her I would be more cooperative. The moment I walked into her stuffy office, her smile was like that of a madman: wide, queer, and seemingly all knowing. She was excited and began asking questions. My answers were short and vague, but she didn't seem to mind.

I made myself sit up so I wouldn't fall asleep, and I fiddled with the silver tissue box. I tried to vaguely explain why I ran away, tried to get her to identify with my sense of adventure without alluding to my plans to run again. She smiled, nodded, and took notes. She seemed to almost identify with what I was saying, and I felt an awful, unsettling peace. Maybe there was something wrong with me.

Before I left, my shrink gave me a prescription for antidepressants, but I wasn't sure if I would ever try them. I waited outside on the manicured lawn for my stepmother to pick me up. I was disgusted at the relief and ease I felt after talking to my shrink. I had to convince myself that it wasn't me, it was my family, or my plans would be ruined. I pulled out strands of the green and wanted to turn off my brain. I knew I was hurting my dad, but until now I had never really felt bad about that.

When my stepmother arrived, I quickly got into the car. I hated that building; it pulsed with the practice of brain washing. I decided that it wasn't me; the shrink had tried to trick me into thinking I had issues. I had better things to do than contemplate her head trips.

"Why am I not dead?" I yelled as loudly as I could, disturbing the calm silence and making me painfully aware of my loneliness. *I must be a fucking moron. I can't even kill myself!* Rolling my wrist at my side, I could feel the thick layers of dried blood crack and flake. I couldn't force myself to look at it. I was afraid to confront the damage I had done—or didn't do. *Why didn't I die?* It's not like anyone would care. Engulfed in a self-administered infection, I festered and began again to cry. But there, in the distance, caught between my sobs, I heard the wailing of a train whistle. I listened religiously, afraid to breathe as the thought sunk in. *This shy girl? Could I be so bold? Would I make it?* Something in me was suddenly changing. I felt reborn. Taking in my first breath, I was to myself confident, brilliant, and beautiful.

I held my arms out to embrace the world, whispering to my soul, "It's not me, and it never was." I knew then that it wasn't up for debate. I was running away. Tomorrow I'd leave, reinvent myself, and shape my own destiny. For the first time in my life, I didn't feel numb.

"Fuck this town!" I yelled, getting to my feet. I fought the blood loss dizziness and beheld the town I'd never call home. I noticed the almost black drying blood on my jeans, t-shirt, and the sad flannel jacket spread at my feet. I became nauseated at the sight of the deep canyon carved in my wrist.

"Gross," I said, holding the dripping cut away from my body. I inspected the plump, yellowing cells from a safe distance. I'd never realized that there was that much fat in my wrist. It bled slowly, absorbing into the dirt. "I don't have time for this shit," I said. I ripped the sleeve off my t-shirt. I had plans to make and bags to pack, so I wrapped my wrist as tightly as I could and carefully put on my backpack. I put pressure on it to calm the bleeding as I walked home, examining the in-depth details of my escape.

School must be out, I thought, seeing the bus full of kids drive by. For any other kid, the principal would call to inform their parents that they weren't in school, but he didn't ever call my house. It was a small town, and I think he must have known what my parents would do to me if he told them.

When I got home, I used my backpack to hide the blood on my clothes. As I headed down the hall, my mother called after me, "Did you fail anything today?"

"No, but I do have a science test to study for."

"You're going to study?" she said, surprised.

"Yeah, I'll make you proud!" I said, slipping away before she could make fun of me. I went to my room, grabbed some different clothes, and locked myself in the bathroom. Avoiding the mirror, I quickly undressed and jumped into the shower.

I'll leave in the morning and hitchhike to Denver, I thought. *Maybe I'll find a job and stay with my uncle Steve, at least until I've got the money to move on.*

My uncle Steve was the coolest, most interesting person you could ever meet. He was a mechanical genius who could fix anything. He was short tempered, good looking, and had a brain with ingenious problem-solving abilities few could comprehend. My uncle Steve was my favorite person in the world.

I got out of the shower, got dressed, and cautiously moved to the mirror. My face was bruised and sunburned, but I didn't mind so much anymore. There were secrets hidden in my eyes, youth in my skin, recklessness in my heart, and passion all through me.

I opened the cabinet behind the mirror and dressed my wrist with care. I buried my cry for help under layers of bandage. I was sick of crying, and no one would help me but me. From now on, I'd be in charge of my life and the way I felt.

Putting the gauze, pads, and tape back into the cabinet, I accidentally bumped my mom's lipstick into the sink. I held it in my hand a few seconds before I decided to dab a little on. It looked good, so I added a little foundation, eyeliner, and shadow. The effect was dramatic, even though I hadn't put much on. I looked gorgeous! I suppose if Vincent van Gogh could paint *Starry Night* with a little paint, imagine what a girl could do with a little makeup. I smiled at my reflected image and spent a few moments adoring my newfound self-esteem before leaving the bathroom.

I'll never be ugly again, I thought, shifting my mind from the mirror to my travel preparations. I dumped everything out of my backpack and onto my bed. Then I saw David. He lowered his book to look at me. I could see the astonishment wash over his face. I had changed, and David could tell I was no longer the underdog.

"I've got a big science final I need to study for. Would you mind letting me have the room for a few hours?" I inquired.

"Sure," he said, standing up and staring a few moments before leaving the room.

Needless to say, I was flattered. It was the first time it didn't pain my brother to look at me.

I began looking through my clothes and picked out my favorites, stuffing them into my backpack. I was startled when I glanced toward the doorway to discover my family staring at me. Upon recovering from the initial fright, I became part of the awkward silence. I was speechless. Their eyes fixed on me for a few seconds, which seemed like an eternity. They retreated in whispers, and I was left feeling interrogated without a word being spoken.

I refused to dwell on the intrusion and began to pack, pushing away insistent thoughts. *Why did my appearance mean so much? Love could never be farther from blind.*

Sleep was impossible; I just lay there, excited and scared to death. A million thoughts at once were tattered and set astray, incomplete but free to dream. These emotions were sharp and overwhelming, beautiful in the way they made me want to cry. I wasn't numb anymore. I had never felt so alive in my life.

I finally gave in to sleep around four in the morning, only to wake at six thirty. I couldn't remember a more beautiful morning. The whole world seemed to hold me up so that I might fill my pockets with fading stars and rays of rising sunshine. The world would be mine from then on.

I made my final preparations and smiled my good-byes. Walking to the highway in the lazy light of dawn, I felt drunk with thoughts. Reaching the highway, I confidently put out my thumb. I felt calm and deep but at the same time reckless and electric. My heart raced in rhythm with the passing cars, and everything seemed to dance in harmony. The breeze caressed and held me safe like the mother I'd forgotten. Its touch reassured and encouraged.

It didn't take long before a white pickup truck pulled into a nearby vacant parking lot and honked. My stomach fluttered wildly, and for a moment I could only think in colors. Working to find my composure, I noticed the truck was dented, and in places the rust had eaten through the body. As I neared the truck, I could make out the driver, a woman with shoulder-length, wavy, blond hair. She looked to be in her mid-twenties. The closer I got, the more beautiful she became—fair skin, blue eyes, and naturally blushed lips.

"Where ya' goin'?" she asked, hanging her head out the window.

"Denver, or as close as you can get me," I replied approaching her.

"Hum," she muttered, thinking for a few moments before saying, "Hop in!" She leaned over and unlocked the passenger-side door.

"Thank you so much," I said. I walked around the front of the truck and got in. "If it's out of your way, I could find another ride. It's not a problem." I pushed my backpack to the floor.

"Nah, don't worry about it. I'd feel personally responsible if anything bad happened to you," she said with a smile. "Plus, I haven't been to Denver in years. It sounds like fun." She pulled out onto the highway. Canon City faded away, and I felt so relieved. I silently vowed never to come back.

"My name is Anita," she announced.

"Christy."

We talked enthusiastically on the drive. I'd never talked to someone for that long without getting bored or lacking things to talk about. She was a wonderful person and seemed to enjoy my company as well.

Like Pandora's Box, my mind had been opened; it was their curiosity that was my undoing. I was weighed down with thoughts in my father's back yard, watching the tree branches yawn in the breeze. *Why do I run away? Is it from them or from myself? Am I depressed?* I didn't know. I didn't seem to know much anymore. I stretched out on the tufted grass and tried to wander the blue above me. I knew they loved me. I only hurt them. Was it because I never knew my real mother, like they seemed to think? How could I miss a stranger? Maybe it was my childish resilience that kept me blind from the things afflicting me. All I could be sure of was the sick feeling in the depths of my stomach. My deliberation had made me ill. Everything was eating me; I couldn't sort anything out. I had drowned in my problems and confusion.

I should have been doing my homework, but I didn't want to think anymore. I went inside and sat in front of the television watching sitcoms to disconnect me from me. I tried hard to fade away, but my thoughts were relentless and insisted on breaking my spirit.

Anita was a phenomenal artist; the drawings she shared with me looked more like perfected photographs. She was an art therapist and perceived the world with love, creativity, and possibility. Her two daughters (who were on visitations with their father) looked exactly like her—beautiful. She fell in love easily and was often hurt, but it never seemed to faze her. She never stopped loving wholeheartedly.

When we arrived in Denver, Anita treated me to a tour of the Denver Art Museum and lunch. Using the convenience store's phone book, I found my uncle's address. Anita drove me to his house.

"Do you need anything, honey?" she asked as I opened the door.

"No, you've already gone far beyond all expectations," I answered. I got out and secured my bag to my back. "Thank you so much."

"Nah, I should be thanking you for giving me an excuse to go to Denver. I had a great time, and it couldn't have been with better company!"

"Bye," I said and closed the truck door. "I hope you find Mr. Right."

She rolled her eyes playfully at my comment and waved as she drove away. I stood for a few moments reminiscing before I heard a familiar voice behind me.

"Christy?"

Smiling, I turned around to reclaim my favorite person, Uncle Steve. He stood in the open doorway with a puzzled look across his face. I ran to him and wrapped my arms tightly around his waist for a long-awaited hug. I hadn't seen him in almost two years, but he still smelled the same: motor oil, cigarette smoke, and intelligence. His smell worked like catnip on me. I became happy and silly, no matter how bad things were. I began to tear up, so I released him.

"I ran away from home!" I announced before he could ask.

"I always thought you might," he said, smiling. He invited me in. "I've got something for you." He wandered into his bedroom. I could hear him rummaging through his stuff, cussing. His house was like a museum, only with no particular order. Nothing was ever dusted, and everything was tightly packed. Shelves and end tables were covered with model airplanes, trains, and boats. Much larger

RC planes hung on the walls, along with more clocks than a person could count in an afternoon. The coffee table, floor, and desk were covered with parts to only Steve knew what, with an elusive guitar here and there. A lathe rested on the far side of the room next to the kitchen doorway, and a band saw sat in the corner. Not the average living room, but comforting to me anyhow. When he emerged into the living room, I could see him carrying a bottle. "It's the first ship in a bottle I've ever made," he explained as he handed it to me. "I thought you should have it."

"Oh my god, how cool!" I exclaimed, staring into the bottle. "Thank you! This is the coolest present I've ever gotten." I hugged him briefly and went back to looking at the ship. It had been erected in an old beer bottle and painted with precision and care. The large white sails stood tall, and it looked as though without its glass encasement a slight breeze might make it sail away.

My uncle and I spent the next several hours talking and joking around. It felt so good to be with him again. I memorized his every step as he worked to restore an antique grandfather clock. As ten o'clock rolled around, Steve put the pendulum in motion and closed the cabinet. Sinking back into his chair and relaxing from his hyper focus he realized like a revelation: "I'm hungry."

"Me too." My stomach growled.

"Why don't I go out and get us something to eat? You go ahead and kick back on the couch and watch TV."

I channel surfed while my thoughts evolved. Steve would never tell on me. At one point I had tried to get my parents to let me move in with him. I now came to the upsetting realization that my uncle's house was the first place they'd come looking for me, if only out of legal obligation. I couldn't stay; I'd get Steve in trouble for harboring a runaway. But where was I supposed to go? One thing was very clear: I sure as shit was not going back there.

Before I could dwell on it for too long, my uncle came home with hamburgers, fries, and soda. The smell filled the house so I could almost taste it.

"You wouldn't believe what happened," he exclaimed as he handed me food. "I asked for regular soda, but they gave me diet.

I said I wanted cheeseburgers, but they were out of cheese. And to top it all off, the goddamn fries were cold!" He took a bite of his hamburger and ranted on, "Oh, I was pissed! I had to go back and get those stupid fucks to fix it. God, I hate fast food employees!" He took a deep breath and shook his head.

I couldn't help but smile. There was that short temper I loved. "What a bunch of dumb asses," I said with a giggle.

"Well I guess we'll have to eat food made by dumb asses!" He smiled.

Aware of what disgruntled fast food staff were capable of, I discreetly checked over my food, keeping a mindful eye open for spit or other undesirable additives.

After dinner and TV, my uncle gathered a few pillows and blankets and put them on the couch.

"Put this in your bag in case your parents come to get you." He handed me a wad of money. "I'd like it if you didn't run, but if you have to, I couldn't blame you. Take that money, and keep in touch." He kissed my forehead and went to his room to sleep. I fixed the couch into a slumbering paradise and by the sound of the television fell asleep.

I couldn't sleep, so I sat quietly on the back porch. The whole world seemed to be moving and changing, but not me. I stayed the same. My bag was packed, but I couldn't go, and I couldn't make amends with the world or myself. How the hell did this happen? I had everything figured out, myself and the universe, but now I was so confused. I couldn't leave because I had issues.

Staring at the waxing moon, I could feel that its company had left me. It belonged to someone else now. Everything but me glimmered and shone in the silver hue, and the cool night air held me. I closed my eyes to feel it saturate me with its melancholy mysteries. In the distance, I heard the wailing of a train whistle beckoning to me. "I can't go," I whispered to the world, and my eyes burned with the apology.

The next day I watched with passionate attention as my uncle worked on a Harley in his shop. It was the most amazing thing I'd ever witnessed. Every movement was precise and meaningful. I swear, he could have put the whole thing together blindfolded. As his hands worked with the bike, I knew what Michelangelo must have looked like carving David. I was in the presence of divinity. Hour after hour, I could not disentangle myself, nor did I feel the desire to. I was given the honor of handing him tools and helping when he could use it.

We ate dinner at Tortilla Flats and spent the evening walking around Denver. After our feet had blistered and we had consumed enough peach ice cream to kill a horse, we walked home.

I lay on the couch that night hoping my parents had forgotten about me. I knew the absurdity of such a hope, but I was ready. All I would have to do was grab my backpack and split. I had neatly packed my bag, wrapping the ship in a bottle in my spare clothes to ensure it wouldn't break. Then I placed the bag on the coffee table. I still hadn't the faintest clue as to where I would go, but anywhere would be better than Canon.

My daydreams melted into my night dreams, and I soon discovered myself soundly sleeping. My mind's unconscious journeys were thick and sweet with fear and possibility. I wanted to stay a while, but I woke suddenly. Feeling scared and uneasy, I got up and walked blindly to the window. I spread the shades to peer out to the shadowy street to find it quiet and lonely. There was no relief; I still felt terrified. All I could do was stare and wait. Minutes passed, and the feelings grew worse. Finally, in an apex of terror, my parents' brown, chipped station wagon pulled in front of the house. My stomach turned in tight knots. I was frozen. I felt a rush of self-hatred and frustration. I watched in slow motion as my parents got out of the car and headed toward me.

"Not without a fight!" I whispered, whipping around. In an insane, adrenalin-fueled drive, I grabbed my backpack and sprinted toward the back of the house. With only a few feet to freedom, I tripped over a short filing cabinet and crashed to the floor. I quickly struggled to my feet just as the doorbell rang. My stomach turned, and I stumbled the remaining distance, yelling, "I gotta go! I love you, Steve!"

I flew out the back door, across the overgrown yard, and down the alley. I felt the cold night air, and the darkness covered me with security and hope. With nowhere to go and no one to keep me company, I ran, turning down no-name streets. With the sound of footsteps behind me, I became panic stricken and disoriented. I ran faster, but the footsteps drew closer still. The streetlights became fewer and farther apart, and the dark overwhelmed me. I couldn't see where my feet were falling, and I couldn't help stumbling. My muscles were giving out, threatening to fail me. I felt like I was suffocating.

Suddenly, like a match in a pitch-black room, the lights of a railroad crossing sign began flashing. Feeling like a lost sailor finally beholding harbor lights, I pushed on to conquer the remaining fifty yards. The train pulled onto the street and down the track like a Chinese dragon with continuous cars like yards of fabric.

I sprinted down the street to meet it at its side, watching as it moved with heavy grace. I was humbled by its quake. My body shook with exhilaration, and my heart drummed to its orchestra of rhythmic sounds. I stood entranced for several moments, and then, without a single thought, secured myself to the ladder welded to the train car. As I was carried away, I looked back to the empty street, wondering if my pursuer was factual. I held on, trying to catch my breath along with reality.

The train headed out of Denver. The car jerked forward with its increase in speed. I was taken by surprise, my feet slipped from the ladder rung. I dangled helplessly from perspiring hands. My feet were kicking in a desperate search for something to step on, and my backpack lusted for gravity. My eyesight blurred, and the world became obscured and distorted. I was falling, but as if in a dream someone grabbed me and pulled me to safety.

Chapter 3

I felt her slip even before I knew she was there. With my heart racing, I tried to recap the last few seconds. I had been sleeping when I woke suddenly with a girl apparently fastened to me as simply as you would have a button on your jacket. For a lack of better options, I had pulled her on top of me. Becoming embarrassingly aware of this fact, I quickly sat up and apologized.

She stole a few quick breaths before excitedly yelling, "Holy shit! You saved my fucking life!" High on adrenalin she laughed, cussed, and shook involuntarily. "I owe you everything. Thanks." She settled in next to me, shaking, smiling, and giggling.

"My pleasure," I replied, watching her.

She smells like summer, I thought. I pulled a candle and lighter out of the front pocket of my bag. *Not that summer is such a simple smell. Like dusty roads, afternoon rain, peanut butter and jelly picnics, watermelon, and swimming pools.*

"So, what's your name?" I asked.

She paused and looked to the sky as if asking the moon for her name. She smiled and then replied, "Echo. Call me Echo, cuz I hate my real name."

"Well, Echo, we are fortunately met. My name is Bon." I held out my hand.

She laughed and shook my hand. "Like Bon Jovi? I love it. Is it your real name?"

"Yeah, but it's after Bon Scott, dead singer of AC/DC."

She smiled. "What a cool name. I wish my parents had given me a cool name.

"Why Echo?" I asked

"Greek mythology. Echo was a storyteller who crossed Hera and fell to tragic love." She looked almost through me. "She was a storyteller like me."

There were questions I wanted to ask, but I didn't feel I had a right to be so intrusive toward a stranger. Was she tragic? I could sense she had more cause to be here than I did. "A storyteller, huh? Fortunately met indeed. Train rides can get quite boring."

Her smile widened with this compliment, and she sat a little taller.

We sat side by side with our backs against the coal car. I watched the starlight play across his round-rimmed glasses and had to remind myself to breathe. His company held me in oceans of celestial mysteries and silently whispered the lost secrets of falling stars. He lit the candle and cradled it as he placed it into a tin can then set it between us.

Growing up, I'd always had the feeling I was looking at the world through a window, not that I was actually a part of it. But now, with the wind in my hair, as if devised by destiny came the most bizarre of emotions. We were all the world. The whole world seemed to stop and yield itself to us. I had to pinch myself to be sure

I wasn't dreaming. In this perfect moment, we spoke like old friends, with a sense that we had known each other before. We stayed up all night, talking, telling stories, and wondering at one another. For the first time in my life, I didn't feel alone. With the coloring horizon, we accidentally fell asleep. The two of us cuddled under his blanket, dreaming of what tomorrow would bring.

The sun crept higher in the sky, but we could pay it no mind till it was overhead. Bon made breakfast of flat soda and bubblegum, and we toasted freedom.

"Where you going?" he asked with more care and attention then I had ever been paid.

"I don't know. Just away, I guess," I answered with a shrug.

"Well, where have you been?

Ashamed, I confessed, "I've never been out of Colorado." I could see excitement seize him.

"With your consent, I'd like to show you some of the cool places I've found. That is, if you don't mind having a travel companion." He smiled intently, awaiting my response.

"I'd love that." I smiled back, hardly believing my luck. I had been so terrified to go alone, and now I wouldn't have to.

Bon wasn't like anyone I had ever met. He was perfect. He was both handsome and beautiful, playing on the cusp of manhood. Caught between a child's pretending and a teenager's recklessness, he put butterflies in my stomach. He was well spoken, intelligent, and a little strange. I never figured someone like that would want to keep company with me.

After a few hours, the train began to slow. Bon leaned out to investigate and then looked at his watch.

"This will be a good place to stop," he said, turning back to me. He carefully folded the blanket and placed it into his bag. "Are you ready?"

"As ready as I'll ever be," I said. I crouched to pull my backpack over my shoulders. He made hopping from the train look so easy that I followed suit, but unlike Bon, I didn't land so gracefully. My butt hurt along with my pride. Bon impressively conquered the natural urge to laugh. He was concerned rather than amused.

We abandoned the train tracks for the first dirt road that crossed our path. Amidst pastures and freshly plowed and seeded fields, we made for the direction of town. The wind smelled of dirt and the ancient decay of last winter's slaughter, eerie and strangely still. Bon and I made a game of taking turns kicking a rock up the road, making some fun out of the idle time. The road became smoother and wider, and the country houses steadily grew closer together.

The sun burned the ozone brilliant blue, but burned us pink. We scoured the outskirts of the small town until we found the perfect place: a bridge that crossed over a deep creek just barely within city limits. We carefully made our way down the steep, overgrown bank and took refuge from the sun in the shade of the bridge. After resting awhile, Bon took to thumbing through his atlas, highlighting highways and railways, cross-referencing, and adding an occasional reroute.

I found myself unable to pass up the opportunity to play in the creek. At the creek's deepest, it came to mid-thigh, but that was plenty for playing. Soaked from head to toe, I stole glances of the boy who saved my life. I caught him looking at me, and we exchanged embarrassed smiles then looked away. I couldn't describe him. He seemed to wear his soul all through his skin. Like an angel so beautiful, you feel unworthy admiring him.

After I had worn myself out, I sprawled on the weeds to dry. Lulled by the sound of Bon's humming, I drifted to sleep.

She spoke softly in her dreams. I couldn't understand what she was saying; they were the muffled murmurs of a mermaid, I supposed. What a strange and wonderful wonder this girl was; she who wore freedom as her birthright.

She and I were going to California together. From there I figured we could work our way up the coast, staying wherever we wanted for as long as we wanted, then maybe Canada. I didn't know.

I had decided not to run, but something had called me, and I found myself on a train heading out of Phoenix. If I had stayed, Echo would likely be dead, and I would never have ever met her. Oh, destiny, what a marvel you are.

I had never been anyone's hero before, and I was indebted for the privilege. I felt ecstatic, like I had rescued a lost toy and if no one should claim it, I would keep it—for as long as she'll have me.

I had run away on my own a few times in search of that perfect feeling of freedom. Only now had I found it. An endless string of perfect moments. The flash of young eyes over a shared smile, a yielding earth, and a blind society. I am now an invisible ruler of the world. I hardly knew her, but it was destiny that made her my queen.

I set aside the atlas and stood up, supposing it was a good time to set up camp. I made a bed of the softer weeds that was big enough for the two of us against a cement pillar of the bridge. There, on the pillar, in faded spray paint was an orange rocket ship in a bed of silver stars. *How appropriate,* I thought, sweeping out the wrinkled blanket. *We should sleep well here.*

I tried waiting. She wasn't waking up, and I was bored to tears. I tried waiting some more but couldn't do it. Before I had thought of the possible consequences for waking a near stranger, I found myself kneeling by her side, whispering her name. For moments she stirred without waking, but finally her eyes fluttered open to see me. "Hi. Sorry, I'm bored," I said, feeling silly.

But she smiled and replied, "I was getting bored of sleepin'."

I wiped my eyes and hoped I hadn't been drooling on myself.

"Are you hungry?" Bon inquired, standing up.

"I'm getting there," I responded, trying to recall my bag's edible inventory. I suddenly remembered my earlier play date with the creek. "Fish!" I announced.

Bon looked to the creek, then to me. "Fish?"

"Fish," and I realized then that I didn't even like fish.

"I don't have a hook or line," he informed me.

"That's okay," I replied, kicking an empty jar of fish bait. "There's bound to be lots of line and discarded hooks."

He excitedly approved, and we both scoured the bank for line and lures. Before too long, we had acquired enough to get started. We found a couple of strong sticks and lowered our lines into the creek. Quietly, we waited, trying not to make each other laugh.

"I feel like one of the Little Rascals," Bon whispered.

I covered my mouth to keep from laughing. "I was just thinking the same thing."

After three and a half trying hours, we finally had enough small fish to eat. Bon and I squeamishly gutted and beheaded each nine-inch fish, briefly getting into a fish gut fight. We hungrily placed the fish in Bon's camping skillet. I retrieved a can of green beans from my backpack, poked a couple of holes in it, and placed it on the Sterno stove with the fish.

We eagerly forked at the fish and talked about sushi.

When it was finally ready, we sat on the blanket and watched the sun set. I don't remember fish and beans ever tasting so good, even slightly burned as it was. We took handfuls of traitorously bony fish and green beans, shoveling it to our faces. She grinned, satisfied, her cheeks swollen with food. I couldn't help smirking.

"What?" she demanded, trying to cover her mouth.

I shook my head and tried to lose the smile. She pushed into me, and I managed to whisper, "You're too cute." She blushed crimson.

The rest of the evening, we watched falling stars and spoke softly. Curiosity nagging me, I had to ask.

"Why did you leave home?"

Her eyes glossed over. She tried to say something then stopped. Her eyes searched as if looking for an escape. She took a deep breath and whispered, "I couldn't like me and belong to them." I could see tears at her eyes' edges shining in starlight.

"I'm sorry," I pleaded with a loss of what to say. "Did you know I wasn't going to run at all?"

She smiled and looked to the sky.

"I had made up my mind to stay til I heard you calling to me," I tried.

She looked at me confused.

"I heard you on the wind, and I had to come."

She smiled and put her head on my shoulder. "You're crazy," she giggled.

We fell into dreams beneath our rocket ship.

I woke with the sunrise and for a few moments watched Bon sleep. Reflecting on his question, I remembered the wound that had chased me from home. I untangled from the blanket quietly so as not to wake him and crept down to the creek. I pulled up my sleeve and carefully removed the soiled gauze pads. The cut's healing progress wasn't as advanced as I had hoped it would be. I hadn't been able to keep the wound closed. I stuck my wrist in the creek to rinse the dried blood. The cold water stung, forcing me to whimper. I glanced up to check that Bon still slept, but he was standing next to me.

What shame I felt at that moment. I wanted so much to take it back. Shame on my hand for hurting me, shame on my heart for wanting it. In the gaze of those eyes, I wished I could disappear.

"Oh, baby," he cried stooping to my side. He looked at me, eyes burning with questions, but said nothing. He only put my hand in his and led me up under the bridge. Shuffling through his bag, he pulled out a small first aid kit. "Let me take care of you." He motioned for me to follow as he sat in the dirt. Bon carefully cleaned the cut and announced that I would live. I was relieved—until he said I'd need stitches.

"I can't go to the hospital! They'll turn me in!" I whined with fear.

"It's okay. I'll do them myself." He paused. "It'll hurt."

"Better that way." I calmed.

He got a sewing needle and thread from a small, clear plastic box. I laid my hand across his lap and looked the other way. I kept waiting for the pain, but it never came. I looked at him.

"I can't do it," he whispered.

"Well, I can try, but I don't know what the hell I'm doing," I suggested. He placed the needle on my wrist and sighed. "Please!" I added.

He closed his eyes, said okay, and pushed the needle through. I flinched slightly, and he promptly asked if I was all right. I nodded, and he lined up for the next puncture. It took all morning, but by noon, he was finished. My wrist was dressed, and we were both relieved.

We caught a train that evening out of Kremling, navigating by train whistle and a whim. Towns came and went in a blur of story time and card games. We stopped in a town long enough to trade trains and purchase a recorder and harmonica. By the time we crossed the Colorado border, Bon and I had a few cheesy songs and a plan for a platinum record. I kissed Colorado good-bye and waved away regrets. Bon and I thought it best to get through Utah as quickly as possible, so in Green River we camped overnight and planned to hit the highway in the morning.

We found an old factory with crumbling smoke stacks and figured it would be a groovy place to sleep. We were mistaken. The pigeons made noises all night, and Bon and I were both creeped out. The distant city streetlights cast haunting shadows in the rubble.

Unable to sleep, we played. Vigilantes in the midst of an ambush, cooing coming from all around us, we dove behind cement pillars and threw palm-sized rocks for grenades. While skirting the shadows, the pigeons captured Bon! The fate of the city was in my hands, and I set out to infiltrate their base. I saved my partner, and we managed, by the skin of our teeth, to disarm the nuclear missile. We played and explored the night through with fear for fuel.

When the sun began to warm the morning, we headed for the highway, stopping at a Texaco to get coffee. Well, Bon got coffee; I purchased a bottle of cheap juice, if you could call it juice. We walked, both half asleep. I sipped my strawberry banana juice, and Bon his black coffee.

"Ha!" I yelled, running to the chipped white windowsill of a small newspaper building. There, in bright-yellow skin, was a beautiful banana. "Mine! You want half?"

Bon smiled and looked impressed, "No, I'm all right."

"What do you suppose the chances of that are? Here I am, homeless, walking down the street, drinking strawberry banana juice, and *bam!* There's a banana on a windowsill. That is just too cool!" It took me quite some time to get over the banana sent from God. Bon laughed and shook his head as I went on about it. We walked down the highway, watching for the fuzz and taking turns sticking our thumbs out. Finally a man in an old white camper with Montana plates pulled over to give us a ride.

Bon and I split the passenger seat of the disconnected cab while admiring the rustic, bachelor ambience of the vehicle. Fast food packaging littered the floor and caseless classic rock cassettes lay across the dash. The occasional cigarette butt or Kleenex elusively hid amongst the debris. Oddly enough, the only smell detectable was that of dust and coffee. Our sanctuary went by the name Robert, a free-spirited gold panner. You could tell he used to have brown hair, but now it was mostly snow white. He laughed almost like a child, but with resonant wisdom earned with his age.

We made acquaintances with our new host and anticipated a long ride. Robert was going to Northern California and didn't mind us riding along. We would make good time this way, and we were grateful.

I wanted so badly to see the ocean. It had always fascinated me, with its diversity of life-forms and the absolute beauty of it. When I was little, I had often pretended I was a mermaid living in the ocean. For the first time, I would be able to see it. I felt so excited I could hardly wait.

Having not slept the night before, we did as dreamers should. Echo and I fell asleep passing the long highway hours, cradled safe and warm. I was her father, and she was my mother, best friends and strangers. We were going to raise each other in this crazy world. My last thought was, *What is she dreaming of?*

We quickly grew fond of Robert. He told us fascinating life stories to ease the long hours of endless highway: his drug years and a dog named Coke, an arduous recovery from a motorcycle accident, and life in panning towns. Like a hero in a novel, he won our attention and hearts. Had these fantastic stories come from someone else, I would have had a hard time believing they were factual. Robert was stubborn, honest, and a little crazy. Like so few, he was unable to compromise.

Adopted as our foster parent for the time, we thought it would be appropriate to bicker just to hear him say, "If you two don't knock it off, I'll turn this thing around." Unfortunately, we couldn't find a thing to argue about.

In the numbered evenings we shared with our foster parent, he generously fed us, mainly a bachelor's diet of spaghetti or macaroni and cheese, but one night we cooked hotdogs on a grill in the Wal-Mart parking lot. Turning a blind eye to the queer expressions of the resident shoppers, we gorged on the bounty of nameless animal parts.

The camper had a second bed. Robert helped to rearrange the booth table so Echo and I could sleep in comfort. In theoretical comfort, anyway. Robert's snoring had us laughing so hard it took determination or exhaustion to finally fall asleep.

I kept expecting what I thought was inevitable—the questions. He never asked them. Maybe he already knew we were runaways. Maybe he was just too preoccupied telling us about himself to think of asking about us. He treated us like people, not our parents' property, and it made Echo and I feel important.

Our stop would be Mt. Shasta in California, on account of a lady friend Robert was planning to meet. He had made her acquaintance over the Internet, and cyber chemistry was imminent.

Once we had reached our stop, we found it hard to say good-bye. After all, Echo and I were still babies and needed a guiding parent.

The fragrance of exhaust and hot dogs cooking somewhere was all Echo and I seemed to notice of our new surroundings. The town blended with the dozens of others we had passed through. Our neglect stemmed partially to parting remorse but we were also eager to start the next adventure.

Robert handed us a couple of gold pans and told us that if we struck big, we would have to find him to give him his share. We agreed, took our leave, and were alone again, eager to see the ocean, journeying ever farther from home.

I thought she would cry when for the first time she beheld the sea stretching out before her. She was honored to have the icy saltwater lapping at her ankles. Then we moved south to find warmer beaches.

Chapter 4

Provisions were low, and we had to conserve when we hopped a train in Eureka. For two days we had nothing to eat save for a few stale crackers. As night fell, we were so hungry we couldn't sleep. Leaning against the coal car, we made pictures in our heads, pretending to dream.

Bon sighed and sat forward to fumble through his bag. He pulled out what I thought to be a deck of cards and covered his head with the blanket. *Strange time to consider magic tricks or a game of war,* I thought. When he emerged, I tried to hide the immense shock that tickled all through me. *Act cool,* I told myself. There, tucked semi-naturally between his lips, was a lit cigarette. He took a shallow drag then handed it to me.

"It will help," he said. Since he was the only person I trusted, I believed.

I knew how to do it. I used to watch my mother and begged her to make smoke rings. But I had never tried myself. I took the cigarette awkwardly, placed it softly and barely between my lips, and pulled a little warm smoke into my mouth. It tasted funny but not necessarily bad. Handing the smoke back to Bon, I parted my lips and inhaled. Like the fires of hell, it scorched my pink lungs. I held my breath to stay in control. Eyes watering, I carefully exhaled. Satisfied I had not given away my inexperience, it was my turn again. Unfortunately, I couldn't keep fooling, but neither could Bon. We coughed our way through the rest of the cigarette, throats sore and slightly dizzy. Bon was right—I didn't hurt with hunger anymore. We both were able to fall asleep.

We forced a cigarette breakfast while our eyes searched for signs of a town. Within a few hours, the train began to slow, yet we saw nothing but fields and waited, confused. Suddenly there was a fence, and Bon jumped up. "Shit! Train yard." He threw his backpack on and exclaimed, "We gotta get off, now!" I quickly followed him.

We jumped and briskly began to walk out the direction we had come in. We didn't get far before we heard someone yell, "Hey!" The voice was deep and intimidating. We bolted like an impact tool, faster still but not faster than our antagonist could throw rocks. One deflected off my bag, and another stung my calf. I glanced over my shoulder. A fat, bald man huffed after us, stooping to pick up more rocks. I looked to Bon, but he didn't look so well. Bon began to weave and then stumble, and I grabbed a firm hold of his shoulder strap to steady him. Finally making the last few yards to freedom, we slid down the steep dirt bank of a dry ditch and followed it a ways. Once I was sure we weren't still being followed, I permitted a stop to catch our breath.

Bon's eyes were hazy and tired. He leaned against the steep six-foot bank of the ditch, and I did my best to lay him down softly. Then I noticed the blood creeping down his neck and saturating his black t-shirt. He giggled sleepily and said, "You can't catch me, I'm the gingerbread man." Then he passed out. I freaked. "Bon! Bon!" I screamed, trying to sit his limp body up. The gash in his head was the length of my palm and wouldn't stop bleeding.

"What do I do?" I yelled at Bon as he lay there motionless. *Help. I have to get help.* I left him there and scrambled up the bank to search for signs of civilization. There was a farmhouse at a considerable distance, and I wasted no time. Jumping back down into the ditch, I grabbed Bon's hands and dragged him along on his backpack. My feet continuously slipped in the sand, and my mind raced. *What if he dies? What will I do? This world would hold no place for me if I was without him. What if he suffered major brain damage and thought he was a germ-phobic superhero or a talk show host? Or worse, what if he went home?*

Tears rolled down my cheeks in my anguish. Farther and still farther I dragged my best friend, who was still bleeding and unconscious. Finally, we were close enough. I sprinted across the field and rapped on the door. I then collapsed on the stoop, impatient for an answer. Forever later, a man dressed in a blue cowboy shirt and worn jeans answered. Out of breath and frantic, I tried to tell him of Bon. He didn't understand. I wobbled to my feet. "Help. Please help!" I yelled, motioning for him to follow me. We jogged across the field to the ditch, and he struggled with me to lift Bon out.

The old farmer and I said nothing to one another as we walked quickly back across the field. Bon was helplessly cradled in the man's thick, strong arms. I thought, *What are we doing out here? We should be at home, safe, with our stomachs full.* Yet I could not have regrets. Bon, who was a full head taller than I, looked so small now. Independent as I thought we were, I realized then that we were just babies in a world too big for us.

Once we reached the hospital, Bon was swept away. I sat in the waiting room. Bob the farmer sat down next to me. I thought he had left. He handed me a lemon-lime soda and a chocolate candy bar and asked, "Will he be all right?"

I didn't actually know yet, but the poor man's face was distorted with grief. "Yeah," I said. "The doctor says he'll be just fine."

His face relaxed. "Would you like me to call your folks?"

"Oh . . . no. I already did. But thanks." I said. He looked at me as if reading fine print and then looked down at his hands.

I wanted to hug him, and if I had anything worth giving, I would have given it. This tall, dirty-blond farmer, strong as an ox with a heart of gold, had saved us both—Bon from bleeding to death, and me from losing my mind. I wanted to tell him he was a hero to us, but my shy nature kept me quiet.

"I had best get going," he said, standing. I thanked him for all he had done for us.

Once he was out of sight, I quickly ate half the chocolate bar, sobbing ever so quietly. I placed the second half into the small front pocket of my backpack as a binding self-gesture that I would see Bon again and be able to give it to him. I waited for a long time. I made a game out of how long I could make the soda last.

Finally I was led up to Bon's room and handed a stack of papers. He was asleep in the bed. I took the seat next to him and looked over the forms. I didn't know any of the information required to fill them out, so I gave up and stared at him. Twelve stitches and so many questions I couldn't answer about him. My stomach fluttered at the thought of someday knowing all those little things that make a person recognized by society.

As my thoughts evolved, I became overwhelmed with the desire to tell him about myself. Since he couldn't hear me, I felt there could be no harm done.

"What I wouldn't give to be like you," I started. "I'm a nothing, and until now I've never been wanted. At least I feel like you want me around." I stared at him, waiting for some kind of reply. In his sleep, he sighed dreamily. I smiled, content with his answer. "My whole family is smart, and I've always been a borderline retard. I've never been accepted by them, and I was used as the family whipping boy." I halfway wanted him to hear me. "I tried to kill myself, thinking life would be better for my family. Maybe my parents would love each other again. I just didn't belong. I was lonely in a house full of people; in fact, I've always felt lonelier when they were around than when I was alone. You're the only one who's ever made me feel valuable."

Bon's eyes slid open, and he glanced around quickly before sitting up. He looked into me and smiled like a child in trouble. "Let's go," he said. He stood and filled his pockets with the roll and vegetable sticks from his lunch tray. He picked up the piece of meatloaf, ripped it in half, handed one half to me, and then put on his back pack. I held out the paperwork as he inhaled his meatloaf. Taking up the pen in his greasy fingers, he signed, *Elvis Presley, Memphis, Tennessee*, and tossed the forms across the room. He worked to swallow while checking that the hallway was clear. I ate the tasteless hamburger square, licked my fingers, and hungered for every calorie. I put on my backpack while Bon checked the hallway again. I came up behind him, waiting for the "all clear" signal.

Bon slowly turned around, and I had a moment of confusion. His soft, loving expression sent my heart fluttering. He took up a hand in each one of his and pulled me in close. He bent slightly to accommodate my height. My heart raced. Contact, soft as flower petals and sweet as honey. I became dizzy and felt as though I was in the gravity of Jupiter. When the kiss had ended, we stood with grins, dazed in magic's satisfaction, only to come crashing back to earth with the sound of voices in the hall.

We sprinted down the hall, following the exit signs, taking the stairs and the side exit into the employee parking lot.

Another coal car. You never get tired of the soot. Backpacks full of dumpstered French bread we had acquired behind a bakery. Both of us feeling like fugitives. With twelve stitches in the back of my head and my first kiss under my belt, life was surprisingly wonderful. I felt inspired, in an awesome way, every time she smiled at me. Reckless and responsible, careful and cared for, a lover in love so loved. My heart told me she felt the same, and we knew it was a beautiful way to be alive.

When we reached the suburbs of San Francisco, we abandoned the train and took to foot. I had a rich uncle who lived somewhere in the area. My mother's brother, who barely knew of my existence. Our plan was simple: introduce myself, lie my ass off, and hope he gave us money. A smarter person would make plans to save the money, but this lover planned to spend it on Echo. New clothes and shiny things. Whatever she wanted. I neglected to make her aware of my plans for the money, knowing she would object.

We found my uncle Henry's address in a phone book at a pay phone. We cross-referenced the city map and put purpose to our direction. We made a child's progress, stopping to play all along the way. Left to our own devices and without a chaperone, we made it to my uncle's house in the late afternoon. Happy and covered in coal soot, we stood side by side as I rang the doorbell. Moments later a stranger answered.

"Hello, my name is Bon and I'm trying to locate my uncle Henry."

"Uncle?" the man said condescendingly.

"Yeah," I paused. "My mother's brother." Another hiatus in hope of recollection. "Marie?" At that the man relaxed slightly.

"Hum, I wasn't aware she had any children." He was being exaggeratedly casual, and I knew he just had to be lying. "I'm very busy, so forgive me when I ask, what do you want?" Henry said, shifting his weight to the other leg.

"Well, my travel companion and I have been marooned here. The company we were to have met must have been confused about our arrival date, because they are not here. Out of town, you see. So we were hoping that you could give us refuge until they return." I knew I would be refused if I asked for cash outright.

His eyes were cold like a machine as he lifted his wallet. He pulled its cash contents, threw the bills at us, and replied, "I hope I won't be seeing you again." Then he harshly closed the door.

I supposed I would understand someday. Even though I received what I came for, I still felt so marred and humiliated. My mother had died when I was very young, and I never really knew her. He was supposed to care, that's all.

Too proud to pick up the money, I turned and began to walk away, speechless.

"Bon?" Echo called after me, still standing motionless on the porch. She hesitated and then gathered the scattered bills. I heard the solid thump of her shoe against the door and her sarcastic gratitude. "Thanks, you fucking prick." I couldn't resist. Through my anguish,

I grinned. She counted the bills as her feet pattered quickly to catch up to me. I could only study the ground to keep from crying.

"Woo hoo! Two hundred and thirty four dollars," she announced.

An awful thought entered my head. Two hundred and thirty four dollars was what it was worth to not know me. I couldn't help it; I sat on the street curb and began to cry. She sat next to me, wrapping her arms tightly around this sobbing fool. She did nothing to encourage me to stop, just held fast. People don't want to hear you cry because they don't understand or don't know what to do. Not Echo. She knew, and she weathered the storm right alongside me, allowing me to be sad while showing me she cared, experiencing her warmth and understanding. I was through crying in just a few minutes.

"Let's get something to eat," she whispered slowly, unwinding herself from me. I smiled and wiped my eyes.

We walked down a main transit road into the city and found a convenience store. A few yellow booths lined the front windows, and I sat down, trying not to draw attention to my glossy, red eyes.

"Nachos or hot dogs?" Echo asked, looking toward the rear of the store. She took a twenty of the uncle money and then curled the rest of the bills into my limp hand.

"Nachos?" I responded, and she hurried off.

I still felt blue but angrier now; I allowed myself to indulge in this less personal emotion. *I got what I wanted,* I thought, placing the money in my pocket.

When Echo returned, she came with not only nachos but a quart of milk. She must have noticed the queer look I gave her, because she informed me, "You're gonna need it." She set down the nachos covered in jalapeños. She giggled then said, "They're good for your immune system." We happily suffered through the nachos, play fighting over the last of the milk.

We set off in search of a place to sleep that night, taking a bathroom break at a huge park we had stumbled across. I found it hard to describe my confusion when I saw Echo exiting the girl's restroom and fumbling to fit several rolls of toilet tissue into her backpack. She was ecstatic, laughing like she was crazy.

"What in the world are you doing?" I asked, feeling her excitement.

"Let's visit your uncle's house again." I knew then what she was conspiring to do.

Under the cover of late evening, Echo and I laid waste to the manicured property. We incorporated a rain dance in hopes of making our hard work more permanent. We pretended to be football players making the touchdown pass up and over the tall sculpted hedges. We stood back a moment, admiring our work.

"That's what you get for fuckin' with us," Echo whispered as she took up my hand in hers.

We walked back to the park we had robbed and wedged ourselves into the spiral tube slide. The slide became almost flat before sharply descending to the bottom, and we slept there feeling justified. Sometime in the early hours of the dawn, we woke to our sliding out of the end of the tube, startling an old man walking his dog. He cast us dirty looks as we gathered our bags and exited the park, too busy laughing to care why the man was so disapproving.

We took a bus to the BART and went under the bay into San Francisco. Echo was thrilled, figuring it would be the closest she would ever get to being in a submarine.

Echo's eyes were wide, straining to take in the whole city. She was amazed how the tall buildings could block out the sun and drop the temperature so significantly. I was content to follow her as she wondered aimlessly, window shopping and memorizing the expressions on strangers' faces. I had run to San Francisco before and stayed for over two months. I felt confident that I could protect her here. We ate at a Greek café that was also a liquor store. She kept noting how she had never tasted anything so wonderfully strange in her life.

We spent ten bucks apiece to stay in a hostel with showers. Echo timidly clung to me, and I felt proud to be the one she depended on. The hostel receptionist was an old hippie, his long silver hair held back in a ponytail. He seemed distracted, or high, dropping the formalities of our check-in. "Rick," according to his nametag, handed us clean towels and cot linens.

For a hostel in San Francisco, it was relatively empty. Only twenty to thirty people were sharing the night with us. The hostel was six stories tall, but the floors were small. The boys' rooms were on the third floor, and girls were on the fourth. The fifth floor was private rooms. There was a kitchen and showers on the second floor. The ground floor had a community room and reception. It was nicer than the other hostels I had stayed in, but I didn't feel it was good enough for Echo.

I cut my bar of soap in half and gave one piece to Echo; we split up to our gender-specific shower rooms. Thankful I didn't have to share the stalls with anyone else, I enjoyed the hot water for the first time in weeks. After our showers, we exchanged horror stories about how dirty the water was as we washed. Considering surface area, I hadn't realized a child could get so dirty. I felt almost proud that I had.

Echo's clean set of clothes looked excessively baggy as they sagged from her body. I felt a stab of guilt. I should have been taking better care of her, my equal but after all a little girl. I felt an amazing sense of responsibility and silently promised to do better in the future.

The hostel was equipped with a lost and found, for a lack of a better term. Clothes that tourists and backpackers had left behind (it being rare they should return for them) became donated. The articles were washed and thrown in cardboard boxes, which were placed in a storage room with a changing screen. Echo and I took turns trying on only the strangest of arrangements. A pink puffy skirt and a green skin-tight Mr. T t-shirt were adorned with a black, shedding feather boa. It was well worth it when Echo went into hysterics the moment I emerged from behind the screen. I played a transvestite bent on giving her a makeover. I chased her around the room until she broke the game with a kiss. Echo tried a huge pair of slacks and rainbow suspenders over a Hawaiian Santa t-shirt. She looked quite cute, but I said nothing. Ten to fifteen outfits later, we had made up our minds. Echo was very fond of a worn Fraggle Rock tank top, the rainbow suspenders, and a pair of boys' faded blue jeans. She said she loved the Levis due to the fact they were so long she could wear them as socks too. I chose a pair of orange-and-brown checkered golf slacks and a black a-shirt with spilled bleach down the left side. I finishing it off with a tan cowboy work shirt with black pinstripes.

Wearing our new clothes, we felt more at home in this crazy city.

Chapter 5

I hadn't noticed I was losing weight. The girl part of me was happy, but the tomboy in me told the girl part to quit being such a superficial tapeworm contestant. Bon liked me for me; his smiles would feel the same no matter what I looked like.

We cashed in on the huge pot of spaghetti someone had left in the kitchen of the hostel. We filled our gold pans and took them up the dimly lit, narrow stairs, through the disconnected fire exit, and out on the hostel's roof. We cleared the pans and watched the spectacular city sunset. The gray roofing changed colors with the sky while Bon and I wondered at the random pipes and copper wire that protruded. We piled our dishes and dangled our legs two stories above the power lines in the alley. We stayed till it was dark, shivering through smiles.

We hung out in the common room, hiding behind a couch to read comic books. The other people were oblivious of our presence, and we eavesdropped on their conversations, making smart remarks under our breath, laughing silently. Every once in a while, someone would become wise to us, but they left us alone, figuring we were crazy.

I wasn't too keen on sleeping in the same room with a bunch of girls I didn't know. I had never so much as stayed the night at a friend's house. We stayed up till everyone had gone to bed. We curled up in a corner of the hall, just beneath a window. There we slept through the night, waking in the early dawn to the sound of pigeons on the window ledge above us. We each took a needless shower just because we could before leaving the hostel.

Bon seemed set on spending the tainted money. We enjoyed a few overpriced, tourist-trap museums, and dined out at strange foreign restaurants. Bon even treated me to checkout-stand jewelry. I tried to discourage the frivolous spending, but we were having too much fun, and I looked far to dazzling in my new jewelry set. The money only lasted a few days, and then we were back to where we started.

Thrilled to hold hands like little lovers do, we walked around bumming money and getting lost on the subway and bus networks. We settled on some steps belonging to a shopping center and decided to try panhandling. I took up the recorder, Bon the harmonica, and we played our platinum material. Using Bon's cooking pan, we brought in ten dollars our first hour. Then we met a lady who used to be addicted to crack. She shared with us her wisdom, saying Jesus had saved her and suggested we find him too. She bought us tacos and gave us five bucks.

After our lips had long since gone numb from playing and boredom set in, we left to find our next adventure: finding a place to stay the night. We took the bus to Haight and Ashbury, pretending to be hippies. We walked to the park, intent on hugging the trees and looking under picnic tables for Jesus. We followed the trails deep into the park, scouting for a place to sleep. It seemed all the good real estate was already inhabited or had been recently, so we pressed on. What seemed like ages passed. We found a staircase down a cliff face, and we couldn't resist. We followed the steps down to a flattened clearing in the cliff side and excitedly agreed this would be the perfect spot. We figured it would be safe, knowing none of the crazies would bother to walk that far, and we would be awake before morning joggers could get that far into the park. Bon cooked Rice-a-Roni over the Sterno in his mess kit while we sang the television jingle. "The San Francisco treat. Ding! Ding!"

I did not sleep. I lay awake wondering what axe murderer might reveal himself during the night. My imagination went wild with every sigh of the wind, bird, or bunny in the shrubbery. So I wrote in the dark, a story of some terrible, drug addicted, were-creature. The beast ran wild in this city killing at will, the old and young alike. In the story's final conclusion, my beast fell prey to a religious cult and was forced into rehab.

We spent our one-month anniversary there on the cliff side with two delicate chocolate cupcakes and sparkling cider to celebrate. Strange to think I had been away from home so long yet couldn't miss it. If I was alone, I think I might have been able to, but Bon was all the home I needed. We toasted the moon with our plastic cups and wondered where we would be had we not met. Our conclusions on the matter were not exceptionally desirable.

We seemed to fit in this city; no one said much of anything to us or bummed our change. We were dirty, transient, and happy as loons. Bon and I did as some of the homeless do; we talked to ourselves or made nonsense at one another. People often think that crazy is dangerous, and insanity is intimidating. It kept the even stranger away from us.

Bon and I often liked to watch the seals while panhandling Fisherman's Wharf. We would pretend to be oceanographers studying the lazy creatures as they sunbathed. They reminded us to take pleasure in life. If our needs were met, we could enjoy a stretch and a nap in the sun.

We spent another month in San Francisco, panhandling and saving money. We had nearly three hundred dollars, which we kept hidden in our socks. The big city life was incredibly easy, as long as you didn't mind being homeless. People were generous with us, supposing our parents didn't care. We spent endless afternoons walking about the productive people, playing our music and bumming change for sugar. I found an old battery-powered radio someone had discarded in a downtown trash can. We picked up new batteries, and Bon took it apart and cleaned it to get it working like new. We were a family after adopting and naming the radio Azazel.

A nightmare of the tangible kind aided in our decision to leave San Francisco. As we slept, sometime in the night a predator came searching for us. I woke to Bon shaking me with a finger to his lips. We army crawled to the cover of the brush. I followed silently, somehow aware of the situation's severity.

A large, teetering, presumably drunk man made his way down the stairs. He called to us in a slurred hiss.

"Hey kids, I know you're down here." He reached our camp clearing. "I got some candy for you."

On our bellies, we slid backwards, keeping our eyes on the intruder, inching farther down the steep cliff ridge. We could make him out in the moonlight, swaying slightly then shaking his head to clear his vision. Even in the moonlight, the man's face looked red. I could clearly make out the drool collecting in the corners of his downturned lips. We held still, terrified, as his gaze studied our general location. I held my breath. The man took a lazy step toward us, and I nearly shrieked. I looked to Bon, expecting his fear to mirror my own, but he was smiling. I was then more confused than scared.

"San Francisco police," the man stammered. "It's all right. Come out." How stupid did adults think we were? "I'm not gonna hurt you, I just need to ask you a few questions."

Not by the hair of my chinny chin chin, you freak, I thought.

The man stumbled around, kicking at our bedding and backpacks. "If you don't come out, I can't give you money," he yelled in slurred speech. When we failed to reveal ourselves, he proceeded to urinate on our bed. Bon attempted to stand up, but I caught him in my arms. I could feel his body shake with rage. The man had a good laugh then headed back up the stairs, but we stayed put. Bon and I cuddled and whispered in the darkness, not attempting a return until the light of day.

We went to the Laundromat in a fury that morning. I had a hard time believing that the man had once been someone's helpless baby. What kind of world were we living in? Bon and I started stringing a trip line across the stairs when we slept, but still we weren't able to sleep through the nights.

Those trains began to call to us. Full of the big city and hungry for the lull of warmer, more secluded beaches and safer sleeping, we ventured south through no-name towns along the coast, avoiding the tourist traps.

"The water is warm!" Echo exclaimed with sheer delight. She splashed about as I tucked my socks into my shoes. This would be home for now I figured, reading the thoughts on Echo's face. I tuned the radio to a suitable station before joining her. On our private beach, we danced like no one could see us simply because no one could. Azazel rocked us at full volume to classic rock, and Echo and I competed on lyrical memory.

We found a good-size piece of barnacle-covered corrugated steel and hauled it up to the sand to dry. Investigating the beach further, we stumbled upon a blue, inflatable kiddy pool that was no longer inflatable, a piece of netting, and a rusty, city-issue trash barrel. We also came across a dead seagull but elected to let it alone while our other treasures were set to use. After our articles had dried, we began to work, finding first the perfect place. Under a tall evergreen surrounded by bushes and only moments from the shore, we began to build our house. Bending the steel in a ninety-degree angle around a small tree, which required a lot of clumsy effort on our part, we formed two walls. The barrel laid on its side was suitable for a third while also serving as a place to store our bags in such cramped quarters. As we worked, Azazel chirped along happily, playing Led Zeppelin, AC/DC, and Aerosmith. We draped the kiddy pool over the top, hoping it would be watertight, and used the net for a door. Echo found a white bucket, its past contents now a mystery, and set it in the corner of the shack. "A nightstand," she told me before laying a small bottle on its side atop the bucket. The bottle had within it a little boat with white sails and painted ocean waves. Now it felt like home. Tired and proud, we spent the rest of the afternoon sitting in our shack holding hands and feeling much like we thought others might in their first homes.

I had left my family and home just to choose my own. Here we were in my blue heaven, a little piece of the world for us to share. It was a mix between a child's clubhouse and the realization of a young couple's dreams.

"You know what? Most people would cringe at the sight of this place," Echo mentioned while looking around. "It would seem poverty stricken and dirty, but what do they know?" She smiled at me. "This is more of a home to me than Canon City could have ever been. It's part of the secret world you and I keep between us."

"Always our secret to share," I reassured her.

We would on occasion make the mile trek to the closest town. One afternoon, while dumpster diving, we ran across the town's library. Trimmed with cut stone and built of brick, the humble building stood proud on the corner, surrounded by a meticulous lawn. Tired and hot, we rested in the grass under a shady tree. After taking large gulps of rain water from the jug and recuperating, we elected to explore the library. Upon opening the door, we received a sneer from the librarian. We sometimes forgot the impression two hygienically neglectful children could have. The books were old and dusty, left all alone too long on the shelves. Feeling pity for great works gone to disrepair and neglect, I had a great idea.

"Echo," I whispered, "Find five and bring them back to me." She looked at me as if she were going to ask why but then smiled and nodded. She left me to search, and we spent three hours in the hunt, finally concluding with ten fabulous books misused and unread. Echo followed me, and I found an open window in the corner, out of the librarian's view.

"Go outside and meet me at the other side of this window," I told her, and she skipped off, trying not to giggle. Once Echo was outside the window, I began to slip the books out to her, and she carefully placed them into her bag. Our eyes darted wildly, confirming we weren't being watched. She zipped her bag and turned away from the window. *What a pity*, I thought, eyeing the shelves of books I couldn't take. As I walked out of the library, I ran my fingers across the bindings of the philosophy and poetry books, whispering my apologies.

Echo and I each took one shoulder strap and struggled to bring the books home. Once there, we didn't leave for much of anything. Before too long, we were reading at the same pace, reading to one another, and always beginning and ending the books together. We began with *The Little Prince, Psycho*, and then followed immediately by *A Tree Grows in Brooklyn*. We prayed for rain, giving us the excuse to do nothing but read. With Azazel cooing quietly in the back ground we lost ourselves in someone else's world. *Titus Andronicus* and *Four Quartets*, Aristotle, and *Stanyan Street and Other Sorrows*, talking at length after the sun had lent its last light to the pages. *The Third Chimpanzee, 1979*, and one book that lacked a title and author due to some individual raping it of its spine and cover.

The rain stopped falling so much, and the temperature regularly climbed till heading north seemed necessary. We packed up and spent our last evening with a fire on the beach to celebrate Echo's fourteenth birthday. I presented her with a pair of hot pink cowgirl boots I had run across in a second-hand store. She excitedly put them on and raved about how comfortable they were. They were even a little too big, so she'd have room to grow.

The beach grew cold that night, and under the stars, we felt inspired to make memories. The dark sand felt frozen under our bare feet as we made our way toward the waves. We were alone with the moon and free to dream as dreamers do. The water was warm and melted us into its glimpses of unworldly colors. The moment stole us, and we could do nothing but give in. We were children, unconcerned with appearing grown up. We played. Splashing one another, yelling, and running up and down where the waves broke on the sand. Poseidon would keep this moment of ours perfect as a dream. We waded to our waists, imagining what it would be like to belong to this strange world of water.

How many more opportunities would we get to act silly without feeling so? Growing up so fast, we may never again. I wanted then to stay, forever stolen into one perfect moment. Her hair was damp and glistened in the moonlight, and her laughter got lost in the waves. Those smiles that she gave only to me were more precious than gold. My eyes could see in a pure, uninhibited way, and I knew this was what life yielded that was real. I could have cried, but I was too carried away in our play.

Chapter 6

The hot early morning sun forced us out of bed, our long sighs our protests. We packed our things as if in a funeral hush, our departure looming sadness around us. I wanted to leave but felt sorrowful in doing so. It felt like more than just breaking camp; we were leaving home again.

We made our own quiet good-byes then set out with heavy feet. Slowly the ease came. As the hut faded into the background, so too did the somber grip of our emotions.

As we passed through the town, we dropped three postcards into the main street postal box, knowing we would be long gone by the time they reached our families. I wrote my family of love and apologies, while Echo's simply read, "I'm not dead yet." Echo also sent another to her uncle, short and sweet but far less abrasive. My common sense told me her departure from home was not similar to mine; she had to leave. Her wrist? I felt closer to her than I had anyone else in my life, but did not feel I had a right to ask. She kept her secrets behind her lust for life and delicate smiles. Who was I to dig up her past?

We hit the highway, our bags heavy with books and a new adventure awaiting us. Echo danced with Azazel on the shoulder of the highway, telling me she never got bored with the thrill of sticking out her thumb. "You never know who might stop." In our case, no one stopped, not for three hours, until a spray-painted blue flatbed truck, a man named Jed, and his dog Princess, did. We made ourselves comfortable on the bed, backs against the truck's cab, while Princess sat inside and drooled out the window. Jed took us two towns in the right direction before we had to find another ride. We gave him *Psycho*; it seemed to fit his misanthropic character. We thanked him for the ride.

Next to pick us up was a mother and her two children, a girl of ten and a boy of around eight. We were permitted to sit in the back of the green minivan and observe the family. The lady was harsh while speaking to her daughter while lavishing affection on her son. When we were let out another town over, Echo slipped *A Tree Grows in Brooklyn* into the daughter's hungry hands.

We walked the twenty minutes it took to get out of city limits before putting our thumbs back out. The late afternoon sun made welcome shadows from the sparse palm trees that struggled by the highway.

We hadn't seen the officer watching us from behind the McDonald's billboard. After being brought in three times, I've since been able to spot them long before they noticed us. This one I didn't see until he pulled out onto the shoulder, blocking our path. The squad car was nearly a hundred feet away, and Echo stopped breathing.

"You wanna ride home?" I asked

"No thanks," she insisted. I took up her hand as she whined. "What are we gonna do?"

"Just act like nothing's wrong. Keep walking."

The first time I was brought home, I actually turned myself in because I was cold and hungry in Montana. The second time, I was picked up for shoplifting food, and the third time was because I ran from a police officer when he tried to bring me in for being a vagrant.

I wondered if we'd get out of this one.

As we got closer, the officer stepped out of his car and leaned against the hood. He was probably in his forties, had short, brown hair, and tried to look taller than he actually was. He was in shape and looked as though he could give a fair chase.

I desperately glanced around looking for an easy getaway, but it was all relatively flat. Beyond the few palms to our right, there were rows of grapevines behind someone's barbed wire fence. Beyond the grapes were trees. Across the four-lane highway to our left was another fence and grazing cattle. Our situation wasn't ideal. I was good at hopping fences, but I couldn't become invisible, and there wasn't anywhere to hide. I figured our best bet was the trees beyond the vineyard. Echo had reached this conclusion as well. I could read it in her eyes as she looked longingly toward them. The only pieces of luck we had were that the cop didn't act as though he had memorized the nation's missing persons reports and there was a dividing median, complete with steel guard rails.

We approached as casually as our pounding hearts could let us, and I took a few deep breaths.

"Hello," I called with a wide smile.

"What do you kids think you're doing?" he replied sternly.

It caused me to shiver. That's when the strangest thing happened. Echo, so small and sweet, opened her mouth and lied her ass off.

"Just playing." She giggled, coming to a stop five feet from the cop car.

"Do you know how dangerous hitchhiking is?" scolded the officer.

"We weren't really going to take a ride; we just wanted to know if anyone would stop. Besides, you boys in blue put Manson away a long time ago." She flattered him while batting her eyes.

"Every year countless people wind up missing or dead for doing just that. Now, give me your names," he demanded, pushing his weight off the hood and taking a step toward us.

"Um," I started

"Sara and Danni," Echo interrupted.

"Last names?" the cop said, sounding annoyed.

"Riddle," she quickly followed, and I remembered that that was the name on the last mail box we had passed.

The officer got into his squad car and called in our fake names. We waited by the hood, and I passed Echo a surprised glance. I didn't know she could lie like that. She smiled bright and shrugged.

"You don't look like siblings," the officer observed from his open door.

"We're not. Our dads are brothers," Echo reasoned without missing a beat.

The police officer joined us once again by the hood of his car. "Okay, you guys are off the hook this time, but if I catch you again, you'll both be in serious trouble."

"Oh, thank you so much. I'm already grounded from the TV for not cleaning out the cat box." Echo smiled, and I had to roll my eyes playfully, unable to believe her feminine wiles.

Echo and I walked on, and the cop returned to his clever hiding place behind the billboard. We chattered with relief for some time until we were almost out of the officer's sight. I noticed from the reaches of my peripheral vision his gray car pull onto the highway. He was speeding toward us but hadn't turned on his lights or sirens. I could feel it all through me. We had been identified.

Ever so casually we crossed the northbound lanes, hopped over the guard rails, and then started walking south down the weedy median. As the squad car passed us going the opposite direction, it slowed and Echo smiled and waved as though nothing had changed.

"Hey!" the officer yelled from his open window, and we knew it was time to run.

We sprinted to the siren's sudden wailing. He didn't get out of his car like I thought he might; instead, he sped away from us to find the next crossover. *Duh,* I thought, urging Echo to cross again. Once more we hurdled over the guard rails, dodged a few oncoming vehicles, and ran to the barbed wire fence. I placed my hands on the top of the fence and bounded over before helping Echo to squeeze between the wires.

By the time the cop had made it back to us, he was once again on the wrong side of the road. He elected to try to catch us on foot, parking his car in the median and crossing the northbound highway.

We ran between the rows of ripe purple grapes, nearly reaching the far fence before our persistent companion had tackled the first fence. I grabbed a bunch of grapes and managed to tuck them into the outer pocket of my backpack before conquering the last fence.

Echo and I ran into the trees and were concealed by the thick brush. Dodging, weaving—we just kept running. Starved of oxygen but full of adrenalin, we must have run over two miles before stopping in a thicket of thorny bushes. We stayed as silent as the dead, listening for any indication we had been fallowed this far.

After twenty minutes I pulled the grapes from my bag and offered them to Echo, who was staring out between the brambles. When they finally caught her attention, she looked to me like I was insane and then started laughing.

"Only you would think of food while running from the fuzz," she said before helping herself.

Once our pulses had returned to normal, we continued walking within the safety of the woods until we had gotten far enough from the scene.

We ate a dinner of condiment-soaked hot dogs at a convenience store and arranged a ride with a Bible-banging trucker. He lectured us the whole way to Frisco; we fell asleep to him talking and woke to him talking. We figured it was a mix of loneliness, No Doz, and the Holy Spirit. We felt it necessary to leave *The Third Chimpanzee* in his sleeper and thanked him for the ride. We napped under a rural park tree wondering at how much our subconscious had picked up from the man's sermon.

Upon waking, we discovered a young boy reading at a picnic table across the park from us, and I had to share *The Little Prince* with him. He shyly took up the book and softly touched the cover, smiling. I knew I had found the perfect home for one of my own childhood favorites.

We were once again thumbing by the highway, ready for whatever the world would throw at us.

Before too long we were given a miracle.

"Where you going?" a teenage boy hollered from the passenger seat. Echo and I jogged to meet the miracle blue van. It was a miracle it ran!

"Don't know, don't care, just north," I replied, and the boy seemed to confirm with his company.

"Well, we're on tour, and our next booking is in Redding, but you can come with us back to Chicago if you're looking to go that far."

I looked to Echo. She half grinned and shrugged. "We'll ride," I said.

The sliding door clicked and rolled open to reveal yet another two teenagers, band equipment instead of seats, duffle bags, and bed rolls. We climbed aboard and made ourselves relatively comfortable on the calico shag carpeting. We made introductions with our new hosts: Brad, who was in the driver's seat; Rob, in the passenger; and Kelly and Steven, who shared with us the back of the van. We clanged off the highway's shoulder and were on our way. Kelly told us they were the Stolen Genetics, a band out of Chicago on tour for the summer. They did the usual friendly interrogation—where you from, how old are you, what are you guys doing hitchhiking. We lied, saying we were from San Fran, seventeen, and backpacking till school started again. They eyed us in justified disbelief. Echo was now only fourteen, and I was fifteen and far too naive to pass off our response. They didn't ask too many more questions, only told us about themselves and the underground music scene. They shared over the van's stereo system some of their favorite bands. They were friendly and social, making it impossible not to feel at home.

A band is like a marriage. Love with the same make, of the same genera, and tied together with a BFF bracelet. Lovers of a sound wed under a label, yet they argue and pick at one another. This band was far more functional then my own family, so I decided to pattern after them rather than my own upbringing.

It ate me up the whole drive wondering what lay in the guitar cases—color, style, and brand. I had always wanted to know how to play but lacked the necessary ownership of the instrument. By the time we reached the gig, I felt I would burst at the unveiling. To earn our way, Bon and I unloaded the van into the renovated bowling alley. The lanes had been leveled but were still intact, along with a neon sign of a blue bowling ball and falling white pins. We were instructed to put everything in the office next to the lanes. The building's interior was painted gold with bright-red trim. A spectrum of spray-painted graffiti climbed up the walls in illegible writing. Once we had unloaded the last mic stand, I motioned to Bon to sit with me along the office's far wall. Five feet from the carefully placed equipment, I burned through the last of my patience. Bon smiled at me, one eyebrow raised, as if to question the nature of my intense gaze on the black cases.

"Just wait for it," I assured him as Kelly came into the room. She smiled at us, and I had to pretend not to be interested in her agenda. Kelly unfolded a chair that had been hiding amongst the random debris of bowling equipment and punk-rock paraphernalia. I watched from the corner of my eye as she undid the silver clasps of the long black case. Rewarding my suspense, she revealed a black-and-silver Ibanez five-string bass. I couldn't help it; I stared. Bon giggled softly, and Kelly sat to adjust the tuning.

She must have been aware of my unwavering attention because she finally asked me, once she had finished tuning, "Always wanted to play?" She smiled, setting her bass gently in her guitar stand.

Embarrassed, all I could do was nod.

Her lips drew a brighter smile. "I'll see what I can do."

Bon and I grinned more out of confusion than excitement, not knowing her meaning.

Rob and Steven came in to tune up shortly after Kelly's departure: a red Fender covered in stickers and a Gibson Les Paul in checkered blue with black. They tuned to one another while we watched. Once they were through, they placed their guitars in the stands. Rob handed us two door passes on lanyards that boldly stated, "I'm with the band."

"This way you won't be harassed at the door if you want to leave and come back," Rob told us then left.

"Aren't they beautiful?" I asked Bon, inching a little closer to the guitar stands.

"Yeah," he answered in silly, wistful mockery.

Before too long, more bands arrived, along with a growing line of fabulously dressed teenagers outside the front door.

Thirsty, Bon and I decided to leave while the opening band was setting up. Walking out amongst the hoard of people, I realized the importance of our hosts. Several of the kids were wearing Stolen Genetics t-shirts while voicing their excitement for the show's headliners. We were roadies for a famous underground band. One would think the band would have gloated to this effect.

We stumbled across a grocery store and wandered about the long aisles. Selecting two sodas and a bag of gummy worms, we made for the checkout. People stared as usual, but I didn't seem to mind anymore. I did wonder what they might be thinking, though. Did they only see two dirty kids? With the way I felt, I don't think there was any way the dirt could be all they saw. Bon and I were free as birds; did they feel it when we were nearby? People were often blind to the obvious, but just maybe they could see it.

When we returned to the venue, there were still people lined up outside. A boy told us as we passed, "The show's sold out." We continued toward the door but thanked him for the info. We pulled our passes from our pockets and hushed whispers fell over the crowd of envious kids. Bon and I giggled quietly in the realization of what it must be like to be important. I was in debt to the hospitality that lent us this experience.

It was dark and loud inside, packed wall to wall with thrashing youth. Despite my best efforts, I was terrified and clung to Bon as he clung to me. We made for the office next to the wailing band. The band's members were conversing. There we stayed, awkwardly shy and out of place. After a while the lights came on, and people began changing equipment for the next band.

We left the safety of the office and found a corner so we could watch the show. Lights went down, and they introduced themselves as Lipstick Megacycle, a band from Seattle honored to be playing with Stolen Genetics. Bon and I clumsily bobbed our heads to the beat and smiled out of embarrassment. We slowly inched our way from the corner as we began to feel a little more comfortable. The lights went on, there was another band change, and Bon and I talked and laughed a little louder.

Burn 7 States from Olympia came on, and the lights went down. We slowly inched a little closer. In the lull of a song, Bon tagged my shoulder, saying "You're it!" and he tore off into the crowd. I immediately gave chase, weaving to miss the studded leather jackets and their occupants. Running between fatal teenagers dressed in death metal, I made a peculiar discovery. Those eyes set beneath painted Mohawks and spiked ruin were soft and warm. Gentle smiles with pierced lips were on the girls grinning in their black and purple lipstick. They were dreamers like Bon and I, hopeless lovers and caring individuals. Bon and I need not have felt threatened in their company.

I caught Bon off guard, jumping out in front of him. "You're it!" I said, and then turned and ran. By the time the lights came on, we were exhausted. We sat with our backs against the wall watching the energy of the mass.

Stolen Genetics began to set up, and Bon and I rose to help. Kelly insisted I be allowed to carry out the guitars, and I jumped at the chance to touch them. They were cool like fire's retreat, smooth and heavier than I had speculated. I carefully put each one in its cradle nestled before the drum set. Once we had finished plugging everything in, the crowd became quiet with anticipation. Bon and I joined the audience, exchanging glances and smiles. The lights went out. Like nothing I had ever heard before, Kelly's bass broke through the silence, and I shivered as she was joined by the guitars and drums. There was no dancing or movement of any kind. Everyone seemed to be focused on taking in all that their ears could render them, feet planted firmly to feel the vibrations and dry eyes resisting to blink. As if from misfit heaven, these cherubs lulled the broken angels. I felt like crying. In this moment, we were all united by our hurts and determined to see a better world. The rhythm quickened, and the spell was broken, resuming a more playful environment. We began again our game of tag.

Spending our energy foolishly, by the end of the two-hour set, Bon and I were exhausted. After helping put everything back into the van, we found it necessary to nap. Cuddling amongst the equipment, we dreamed of being underground punk rockers.

We woke briefly at a gas station but refused to start the day so early. We were forced to finally when the van stopped at a coin laundry. We washed one set of clothes, changed into them, and then washed the ones we had changed out of. Bon and I had a lot of time to kill, but Kelly had given us a wonderful way to fill it. After we'd started our first washer, she brought in a small, black guitar case with a treasure inside.

"It's a student guitar, not an electric, but you'll have fun with it," she explained, absorbing our astonished and grateful expressions. We thanked her a million times, and she taught us how to tune it and a few chords. We began putting together a song. The band members politely smiled, but we could tell we hadn't written the next "Stairway to Heaven."

Kelly and I formed a close friendship in the following days. Two shows and many highway miles had yielded my first girlfriend. A comfortable codependency developed, and Bon hid a tinge of jealousy behind his smiles. We always went to the bathroom together and what seemed at first to be very uncomfortable became all too common. I was shocked the first time Kelly dropped her pants to pee while continuing our conversation. I always thought you were supposed to make eye contact when you were listening, but in this case I elected to play with my hair in the sink mirror.

Kelly wasn't like the girls in Canon City. She didn't fuss over her hair or care what people thought of her clothes. She was outspoken and believed in herself. Kelly was a person before she was a girl. Where the girls I distantly grew up with put emphasis on the things they were incapable of doing, Kelly believed she could do it better because of the "disability" of being a girl.

I wrote a story about Kelly, how her uncompromising personality saved the world from a new order of super Nazis. Using music and its underground networks, she built armies to rise up and take the Nazis down. Kelly giggled and blushed when I told her about the story and said she was honored.

Chapter 7

Echo confessed to me several times being excited about having a girlfriend for the first time. I was happy for her and at ease when she smiled, but I inevitably felt lonely, knowing those smiles belonged to Kelly. She had done something for Echo I could never do. When Echo walked, she stood proudly, no longer slouched with shame I couldn't understand. For this favor, Kelly had a place in my heart.

I was relieved when we arrived in Seattle, this being Echo's and my agreed-upon stop. We elected not to stay for the show in order to secure a place to camp. Echo and Kelly made their good-byes, and Echo promised to write. Steve, Rob, and Brad insisted we come out to Chicago to visit someday, and we went our separate ways.

With Echo's smiles all to myself, we walked the city searching. In the remnants of daylight, the rain began to fall, hastening our decision. Echo and I squeezed under a wire fence in an alley leading down to a dry creek to take refuge in one of the two water pipes under the sub-street. The pipe's circumference was barely big enough to sit up in, so we curled short-ways with our bodies shaped like crescent moons.

"So whaddaya think of Seattle so far?"

She sighed and replied, "I love it," with playful sarcasm. "We never got much rain in Canon City, most years anyway." She took in a deep breath. "We'd get some good thunderstorms in the spring, and when I was little I use to sneak out of the house so I could play in them. I'd get soaked." She trailed off and seemed to sink into the grated metal of the pipe. "It made my mom so mad," she whispered.

I could feel the vibrations of her silently crying. I couldn't think of what to say to keep her from her memories. I wrapped my arms around her, and she fell into them. Words I was never intended to hear, drowning in the rain: "Why can't they love me?"

I held her tighter. "My poor baby," I whispered. She gently sobbed in my arms till she fell asleep.

When I woke it was still raining, but something told me not to get up just yet. Instead, I cuddled in close to Echo, singing more softly than a whisper. I would wait till she woke. There seemed to be no sense in rising to the rain when she needed the rest. As the hour wore on, I daydreamed while watching her eyelids flutter in sleep. I wanted to help her but didn't know how, she who was part of me, yet so far away. The flutter of her lids ceased, and I could feel her looking at me through them.

"Sorry for freakin' out." She smiled wearily, her eyes still closed. "Thanks for being someone I can cry on. It means more than you'll ever know." She opened her hazel eyes and placed her hand on mine. "No one's ever cared that much for me."

"I'll always be there to help you pick up the pieces when you fall apart," I said sincerely. We embraced, and I didn't feel so bad that I couldn't fix it. I knew now that all I had to do was be there.

We dorked around, kissing and practicing our songs till the late afternoon, hoping the rain would let up. It did slightly, giving us the chance to make a break.

The hazy light made every hour seem like evening. It was like perpetual TV time, those few hours after dinner and before bed. We lazily walked beneath the tall, shiny buildings, the rain merely a drizzle by now.

Echo gently shivered, reminding me to do the same. Cold and wet, I spotted a coffee shop. It felt like we had stumbled across salvation. I skipped ahead and pulled open the door for Echo. She offered a silly, bashful smile while stepping inside, out of the rain. Our wet shoes squeaked across the thick polyurethane coating the bright-yellow wood floor. We stood back from the counter staring at the chalkboard menu that hung on the wall behind the lady who impatiently tapped her long fingernails on the counter. Echo turned her ankle, making it squeak to the cadence of the speeding cars outside the shop window.

"Let's do a couple of endless cups. Free refills and only a dollar fifty," Echo suggested. She always kept our budget in mind.

"Two cups," I told the cashier and handed her three dollars. Echo pulled a shiny quarter from her pocket for tax. "Keep the change," I noted as we left to fill our cups. I caught the quiet scoff of the barista.

By the eight-foot-tall front window was a long table with an assortment of coffee urns, plus milk, half and half, and sugar. A total of twelve different kinds of coffee.

"We should try them all," Echo joked.

It sounded like a good idea to me. I nodded at Echo, displaying my most excited expression. She looked at me with disbelief then grinned, nodding her head. We started on the left side with 100 percent Columbian. Echo paled her coffee, and we both sat in the same oversized arm chair next to an oak book case. The first cup went fast, with not time enough to finish a Robert Frost poem found in a book hiding on the shelf. A Jamaican drip and another poem and a half. A bathroom break and another cup, French roast and Robert Frost's "Pan with Us." "The Trial by Existence" and a Peruvian coffee. We also read "Lost in Heaven" over a cup of Java jolt followed by the necessary bathroom break.

The ambiance of the coffee shop seemed at our disposal. To clarify, it was perfect for our playful disruption, too much coffee, and intoxicating Frost. People came and went, smiling and pleasantly observing our juvenile caffeine buzz. Business began to pick up, and people of all ages frequented our daycare. In the lull between the next customer yet to arrive and the last clang of the register, I read aloud "A Dream Pang" by Robert Frost. The crowd fell silent, save for the barista and cashier, who clattered dishes in the sink. With the last words, "But 'tis not true that thus I dwelt aloof. For the wood wakes, and you are here for proof."

The people neglected their cooling coffee to comment to one another and make presents of their smiles toward us.

"Thank you, that was lovely," an elderly lady awarded me from the opposite side of the book shelf.

Echo giggled, and the coffee shop resumed its clamor. We returned to the urns of coffee for our tenth cup, vanilla bean. Echo told me, "This is the one I wanted. Had to drink nine cups to finally get to try it. Now I'm so wired I'm afraid I'll dump it all over myself."

We sat back down and retired Robert Frost in order to people watch. Lovers on bar stools playing footsy in the corner, old friends discussing career and family. Lone wolves connected to the world by wire, with cell phones and laptops as attentive companions. Then suddenly, as my gaze rested in front of me, a teenage boy in jeans held out two very small ceramic white cups to Echo and I.

"If you're working for a buzz, these should top you off," he announced and we took up the small cups.

"What is it?" Echo asked, staring into her cup.

"Espresso double shots."

"Thank you," I said in astonishment, recalling their price.

"Payment for perfect Frosting." He left to join a small table of three other teenagers at the far end of the shop.

"Wicked!" I noted, smiling at Echo.

We paced ourselves in the consumption of the espresso and even put away an eleventh cup of coffee. Echo and I decided the twelfth, a decaf, was a waste of our efforts. We didn't leave, agreeing that staying near a familiar restroom would be necessary for a while.

I taught Echo how to play chess, and she picked up quickly to oblige my challenge. Our hands were shaky and became quite the disability. Twice we had to set up the board for a new game due to knocking too many pieces down and not being able to set them back up in their previous spaces. Once the frequent bathroom breaks were not as called for, we left the calming coffee house. Back to the still-drizzling streets.

In search of more hospitable lodging, we wandered the streets in random directions. Stumbling to fortune, Echo lifted a bent and slightly broken umbrella from a street corner trash can. Funny how another's rejected item could thrill us so when conditionally applicable. We basked beneath its function and made good friends, promising to fix it once we had found a home.

We wandered for another rainy day before finding a decent place to call home. Actually our red, blue, and purple paneled umbrella had found it, riding a gust of wind over a fence with a "No Trespassing" sign and bouncing along the tall shrubs and weeds a ways before descending into a creek bed. Echo and I gave chase to find it tangled in a bush with its wooden handle pointing up the creek bed to a short bridge.

Echo pulled the umbrella from the bush. "Thank you," she said, kissing the handle.

What a strange place for a bridge, I thought. It appeared to be paved, and I could only conclude that they must have moved the road. It looked wide enough for two cars and was weathered significantly, implying it had been here for some time.

We walked under the bridge for further inspection. The ground was rocky with pumice and sloped sharply; it was not the most ideal place, but it was dry. Resting in the shelter, Echo made a fantastic discovery. The cement ribs that ran the length of the bridge were beveled at the bottom. If we found boards, we could easily construct a platform that would hug us to the belly of the bridge. No one would be able to see it without going under the bridge itself.

Bon walked under the width of the bridge, stopping under the other side.

"Check this out!" he called.

Upon joining him, I noticed an insulated pipe running along the underside of the bridge. "What's it for?"

"Sewage, I imagine," Bon replied, running his hand along the thick, silver insulation.

"Ew." I turned to leave.

"Wait," he called. I stopped and turned to look at him. "Sewage is warm—this close to the source, anyway." He smiled. "If we build around it, it will be like having a little heater."

We had our work cut out for us. Ditching our bags and guitar under the bridge, we did a quick fix on the umbrella then set off to find building supplies.

"Ya know, Echo," Bon started as we walked, scouring the ground through the thick grasses and brush, "that was quite an ingenious idea." He stopped to smile at me. "I mean it. That was brilliant."

I became ticklish all over, and my stomach fluttered. "Thank you," I managed. I placed my hand over my heart to keep it from jumping out of my chest. We walked on, and I replayed the compliment in my head over and over. *Brilliant? Ingenious?* I had never been called so much as average. My God, I could fly; lacking wings, I did the next closest thing. Grabbing Bon's hand, I stopped and turned him, awkwardly kissing. Stepping back, I blushed, and he closed in, giving a silly giggle and kissing me back.

"No one has ever said anything like that to me before," I said, still holding his hand and resuming the search.

The private property was void of a house or shed or anything. It was, however, beautiful. Small trees grew in clusters, and delicate wildflowers offset the persistent green that covered every inch. There were thorny berry bushes and the thick scent of rainy deciduous foliage. Like a child's forest, it was not big enough for real adventures, but just perfect for playing pretend.

When we reached the far end of the property, we were still empty handed. A road ran along the other side of the fence, and beyond that was an entryway to a residential alley. The houses were small and old, with lawns adorned with either plastic ornaments or rusting car parts. We hid in a cluster of imaginatively heroic trees to scan for onlookers. I let myself feel like Robin Hood for a moment before carefully climbing over the fence.

We walked cautiously up the alley, peering into the back yards of the small houses. There were several dogs, all of which exuberantly jumped at the chance to bark at us. A few blocks from our bridge, we found a large three-story building made of yellow bricks. The windows were filthy, and few were cracked. A small marquee marked the corner entrance.

"VFW," Bon announced, adjusting his glasses.

We walked along behind the building and, to our astonishment, found a tall privacy fence made of old, wide, wooden boards approximately an inch thick, a foot wide, and five feet tall. The thick hedge that grew on the opposite side had already pushed several of the boards off the frame and into the alley, so Bon and I guiltlessly gathered them up. We laid them out on the ground, and Bon had me lay on them to get the proper dimensions. We figured seven feet would be ideal, which meant we should pull three slats from fence. Checking them closely for integrity, we stacked them together and each took up one end. Bon took the lead, and we kept our eyes alert as we hauled home our heavy prize.

Once back to the fence, we slid the boards under and rested, hidden beneath the trees. My arms hurt, but the excitement was an effective distraction. I couldn't wait to get them to the bridge and begin construction. The it was back through our pretend forest to the sewer pipe.

"Oh, they're too long," I complained.

"It's okay," Bon comforted, kneeling to open his bag.

"You got a saw in there?" I asked. I had realized some time ago Bon had packed more practically then I had, but a saw?

"No, though I wish now I had," he said with a playful grin. Retrieving his lighter, he stood to face me. "We'll start a fire and burn away the excess."

"Aw, see, that's why I love you." I helped him search for kindling.

We would place one end of a board into the flame, making sure it burned even and relatively straight. We took it out every once in a while to check the dimensions. One by one, we burned then beat them into place with half a brick we found in the creek bed. We finished in the early hours of morning. The platform was sturdy enough, and we slept long into the afternoon.

With our bellies full of the last of our Pop Tarts, we set back to work. We had placed the platform close to the cement base of the bridge, leaving just enough room for us to squeeze inside. But we were still missing a wall. We set off, not quite sure what we should be looking for, since we had no way of anchoring it into the cement. We couldn't use wood like we had with the platform; it would simply fall out. Maybe a single piece of something that we could wedge in place. We walked for hours, Azazel keeping our pace as we looked for material and asked for spare change. We acquired seven dollars and forty-three cents, along with a half sheet of used sheetrock from a house being renovated.

Once home, we broke the sheetrock into the relative proper shape and size. We pushed the piece in sideways, and then carefully using the half brick, we beat it into place. It wasn't completely sealed around where the pipe exited on the right, but Bon suggested we get a roll of duct tape the next time we were out.

I made ramen noodles for dinner to celebrate. We ate by candlelight and giggled in our second home.

Chapter 8

Echo took to the new place with blazing creativity. She made collages on the walls and ceiling with pictures she found in discarded magazines and newspapers, using bubble gum to adhere them. She found two shower curtain rods at a neighborhood yard sale and, with the help of two metal "No Trespassing" signs, constructed a shelf. She placed Azazel and the little ship in a bottle to one side of the shelf and placed what little provisions we had on the other. The middle of the shelf was reserved for the candle, leaving space to spare.

Before too long the seasons changed, and the trees began to turn colors. Echo didn't want to leave; she was content to brave the winter here. Though Seattle winters were mild, I had always opted for more tropical climates while on a vacation from family. We liked Seattle and, most of all, our new home. With that in mind, we conserved our money and stocked the shelf with dry food, noodles, cereal, and crackers, and splurged on a jar each of peanut butter and jelly.

Our street corner guitar for pocket change was received well. We made at times thirty to forty bucks for a persistent five—to six-hour run. We saved a decent amount of money, but things began to get a little tricky. Once the leaves were gone from the trees, we no longer had the cover to come and go from the bridge as we pleased. We would have to wake before the sun rose to use the deception of predawn. We couldn't risk people wising up to our squatters' abode.

For Halloween, Echo and I made costumes befitting our resources. We went as hobos, purchasing two bandannas that we hung on the end of sticks. Echo drew a black mustache and beard on my face with a washable marker, and we set out to collect free sugar. We figured we were too old to participate, but the allure was far too great.

Starting at the first signs of dusk, we sprinted between houses and covered entire neighborhood blocks in record time. We filled the bandannas and our pockets, and then we resorted to holding out the bottom hem of our t-shirts. We were making better time thanks to our sugar high, so we hit up the wealthier neighborhoods where there were porcelain pumpkins and expensive decorations. They handed out full-size candy bars and the occasional religious pamphlet. We'd eaten so much sugar, we stopped making sense or were talking too fast to make sense. Inevitably, one by one the lights went out, and we made our way home.

Staying up by candlelight, we sorted and traded our bounty while telling ghost stories. I recounted to Echo the ones I had been told on Halloweens past or ones I had read, while she just made them up as she went. To my shame, her stories were better.

As the days grew colder, Echo and I ran out of clothes to layer and decided to pull from the savings to buy a couple of coats. On the bus downtown, we asked an old woman sitting across the aisle where we could find a second hand store. Her ancient eyes sprang to life as though we had given her an important quest. She was delicate and pretty; I couldn't resist imagining that she was Echo in the future, riding a bus to meet me somewhere. The woman's elegant, aged voice told us in detail where to switch buses and what stop to take. I had to stop thinking of Echo while looking at her; I was falling in love with the old woman.

We followed her directions and got off at the third stop. I quietly pondered falling for a grandmother. Was love so strong an emotion that it could transfer like that? Could I love anything while thinking of Echo? We boarded the next bus and settled in near the back.

"You're oddly quiet," Echo mentioned, fingering the hole in the bus's upholstery.

I wanted to share my revelation with her but managed to shove my foot in my mouth. "I fell in love with that old lady on the bus."

Echo gave me the most heart-wrenching look, failing in her attempts to veil it with a slight smile. It was the expression of a deceived angel—angry, hurt, and confused, all beautifully illustrated on a silk canvas.

I quickly found my recovery, my heart breaking with her gaze. "All I had to do was imagine that she was you in sixty years. You were on your way to meet me at a café or maybe to the boardwalk." Her smile drew genuine. "I think I could fall in love with anything thinking of you." I touched her hand softly. "Maybe that's why people can love the entire world. They have that one person to show them how."

She blushed and stuttered on a response. "You love me too?"

I had never told her. I didn't think it was needed, though I had wanted to. "Didn't you know? I have for a long time now." She smiled wide and giggled; I had to say it outright. "I love you, for always."

"I love you too, till time stops," she said, throwing her arms over me and kissing all over my face.

We missed our stop.

When we had reached the Salvation Army (a half hour later by foot), we shook off the cold and began our treasure hunt. We tried on different jacket styles. Most were far too big, but we refused to shop in the children's section. While sporting an oversized men's gray wool winter coat, I posed with my hand in the pocket. I looked toward Echo with astonishment as I lifted from the pocket what memory knew to be a note. Echo glanced around the store and in a whisper said with disbelief, "Twenty bucks!" After that we set out to check all the pockets, despite the curious glances we were given by other shoppers. Our hunting yielded another twelve dollars, a single velvet purple glove, six losing scratch tickets, and countless used tissues. We left the tickets and tissues and gave the rest homes in our pockets.

Echo and I both settled on army-issued parkas with variations. Hers was Swiss, tan, green, and red, with several pockets, a removable liner, and a hood. Mine was camo green, fleece lined, with the nametag "Ash." While waiting in the checkout line, we joked about finding Brownie and Cub Scouts patches to decorate our new coats.

We elected to walk home rather than pay the bus fare. On the way through a run-down district of the city, we came across a soup kitchen serving dinner. We discreetly, with attempted respect, eyed the line of vagrants. The line followed the brick wall of the building. Twenty or thirty poor, hungry people quietly waited with embarrassed eyes. Echo and I were humbled, knowing circumstance had rendered most of them here, while we had chosen to live this way. Grateful our youth made life on the streets easer, handouts were given without judgment. Our own devices were not destructively hindering us. Echo's eyes teared up, and I wrapped my arm around her waist. Dropping our gaze to the sidewalk, we continued on our way.

It was long past dark when we reached home. We shared a block of dry ramen noodles for dinner while laying wrapped around one another on the floor of our clubhouse. Azazel whispered softly as the candlelight danced shadows on the collaged ceiling and walls. We reflected on the crazy day as I studied the pictures. She had transformed shallow models into modest angels with tin foil wings and newsprint gowns. Fable creatures had been pieced together and now walked through cityscapes or classic photographic landscapes. In chopped headlines, letters pasted like a ransom note read, "Bon and Echo, free forever." In places the walls and ceiling were still bare, but with winter steadily descending, I was sure by spring there wouldn't be a bare patch of cement left.

She spoke softly of love, life, and being an aimless runaway. Sometimes, like tonight, I listened so intensely to the sound of her voice that I couldn't hear what she was saying. She didn't mind, so long as I was there to return her smiles and hold her close. I drifted to sleep hoping we could spend the whole winter this way.

Echo cut a small branch from a pine tree and set it up in a soda can in the corner atop the pipe. I collected shiny bottle caps, punched holes in them, and strung them with the fraying fibers of my jeans. She made a tin foil star, and over a hot cup of cocoa, we decorated our Christmas tree.

Within the following few days, we pulled from savings to do a little Christmas shopping. Splitting ten bucks at the downtown shopping center and monorail terminal, we exchanged kisses and went our separate ways. I had given my gift to her much thought and had finally decided. I wandered in search of a book store.

I wanted to get her a journal, a special book in which to write all her stories. Until now she had been using a spiral-bound notebook. The cover had long since fallen off, and the wire binding was crushed. For fear of reaching the notebook's end, Echo had started writing two lines to every one, and I knew her stories were far too good to reside in a tattered notebook.

Once I had found the journals, I couldn't make a decision on which one to buy. There were so many colors, sizes, patterns, pictures—would she want a lock? I spent far too much time scrutinizing my options. None of them seemed to fit her or do justice to her literary efforts. Echo wasn't a pink flower or black leather, not a lighthouse or purple-and-blue checkers. Crestfallen, I contemplated looking for another book store. Finally, I saw the perfect one, set behind all the others, in glossy, sad colors. It reminded me of Echo. The picture was a cityscape with a somber feel, and Echo's smiles always seemed sad to me. Not sorrow like in death, but the feeling that every perfect day has an ending

The journal was twelve dollars, and I felt it only right that I get her a pen as well. I picked out a nice one with a stainless steel barrel, a ball point with black ink. This added another seven dollars to the total, but having anticipated a higher price, I retrieved the extra twenty dollars I had been saving from my sock before heading to the register.

Five dollars wouldn't be enough to buy him the world or much of anything, I thought as I walked through the mall. I wanted to give him a wallet because the boy I loved was becoming the man I would want to marry, and men used wallets while Bon adorably still filled his pockets. I want to be the first to give him a man's gift. I found cloth with Velcro wallets in the neighborhood of five bucks, but I wanted to give him a nice leather one, and those were closer to twenty. How in the world could I get more money? I sat with my head on my hands on a bench just outside of yet another coffee shop. It would take too long to ask for spare change; I was supposed to meet Bon in an hour and twenty minutes. I sighed. Then opportunity knocked. In clear view from where I was sitting, a woman in the coffee shop was scolding her two young children. They were misbehaving, tired of Christmas shopping, and trying at their young mother's patience. I seized the opportunity and entered the shop.

"Hello, my name is Echo, and I'm a storyteller." I smiled at the woman. "It seems as though you have your hands full, and I thought that maybe I could help you out by distracting your children with a story." She eyed me suspiciously and politely tried to smile. Feeling the rejection coming, I intervened. "I write children's stories and am always looking for kids to try out my latest work." The mother relaxed and agreed.

Drawing the children to the closest table, I sat down and began by asking their names. The little girl was Makaila, and her younger brother was Pahn.

"I'm five," the little dark-haired boy told me proudly.

"Yeah, well, I'm seven," Makaila said, and then stuck her tongue out at him.

Before he could retaliate I said the magic words.

"Once upon a time." And the two of them settled in, sharing the same chair. "There lived a little boy named Dhonn. He was lonely because he had no brothers or sisters to play with. After a long morning of playing alone, he asked his mother if she would take him to the park so he could play with other children. She agreed, and Dhonn helped his mother find her keys and purse.

"By the time they reached the park, the boy was so excited he felt like he could explode. He jumped out of the car and ran to the park equipment while his mother sat on the bench to read a book. There were no children. He checked the slide, behind the bushes, in the trees, and even beneath the merry-go-round, but he could find no children. Looking around the park, he saw several mothers with their noses in magazines or books but no one to play with. Had all the mothers not noticed where their children had gone to?"

The two children shrugged with their inquisitive eyes on me.

"Dhonn began to cry, feeling so lonely. Then he heard a deep, malicious growl coming from the behind one of the trash cans. When he looked, he saw a great, big, monster with red, scaly skin and long sharp teeth!"

The children excitedly fidgeted.

"'What have you done with the children I came to play with?' Dhonn asked the monster.

"The monster laughed replying, in a hissing grumble, 'I ate them all up.'"

Makaila and Pahn gasped.

"Dhonn angrily picked up a rock and threw it at the monster, hitting him in the knee. The monster looked hurt, as thought he might cry. 'Now I'm gonna eat you!'"

Their mother gave a scornful glance then turned to order her coffee.

"Dhonn took off running and yelling, but none of the mothers seemed to notice! After the monster had chased him all over the playground, Dhonn knew he would have to be brave. He turned, planted his feet, and readied himself for the monster.

"Dhonn made a fist and punched the monster right in the belly as he charged into the boy, knocking them both to the ground."

The children's faces were relieved and they smiled as their mother moved to loom behind them, her coffee in hand.

"Dhonn got up and readied himself for the monster's next attack, but the monster didn't get up. He lay on the playground quietly, and Dhonn crept closer and closer."

Makaila and Pahn clutched each other, and their mother slipped a little giggle.

"Then Dhonn realized the monster was crying. 'No one will play with me,' the monster muttered between quiet sobs.

"'I'll play with you, so long as you don't try to eat me,' Dhonn said.

"The monster stood up. Big teardrops fell from its' scaly face, and within each one was a child. They splashed to the ground and ran off to play. With every tear, the monster shrank till she was just a little girl and not a monster at all.

"Dhonn was amazed, and the little girl confessed, 'None of the children would play with me, so I ate them up, and it only made me sadder.'

"Dhonn and the little monster girl played all that day and the day after. They became best friends, and whenever a monster appeared on the playground, they knew how to defeat it, together. The end."

The two small children immediately called out, "Tell us another one!"

"But look," I said motioning behind me, "your mother is all done, so it's time to go."

"That was a really cute story. You should see about getting it published," the beautiful mother said, smiling and walking closer to collect her children.

"Maybe one day," I replied as I stood.

She handed me a bill, saying, "Thank you. You've de-stressed our holiday shopping." She shooed her children toward the door, and I looked at my hand.

"This really isn't necessary," I called, stepping toward her and holding out the bill. She just smiled her insistence and left.

Fifty bucks. I was dumbfounded. *This is what it must feel like to sell your first painting,* I thought, overflowing with pride. I walked from the coffee shop wanting to hug everyone I saw, smiling and laughing out loud.

Now I could get Bon one of those nice leather wallets with snaps and a plastic picture insert. And something nice for Christmas dinner. I felt intelligent, beautiful, and invincible. Every time I thought about it, my knees got weak, and I wanted to laugh myself stupid. *Fifty bucks just for telling a story to a couple of cuties. Wow, wow.*

After purchasing a beautiful black leather wallet, I had it gift wrapped at a stand for two dollars. With a smile that could light a crypt, I walked to meet Bon but couldn't resist telling him about my experience. I didn't want to make him feel bad for only spending five dollars on my gift while I found a way to get more for his, so I told him I had already bought his gift and told the story to kill time while I waited to meet him. I told him she had given me thirty-five dollars, and I had used two dollars to get his present gift wrapped and a dollar for a box to put it in.

He was so proud of me and begged me to tell him the same story on the way to the grocery store.

We browsed the aisles for Christmas dinner. I was looking for the traditional meal, but Bon interrupted, grabbing a quart of chocolate milk and asking me, "What's your favorite food?"

Confused, I tried to think. "Seafood and pasta." It was my obvious choice, but not particularly festive.

"Screw tradition!" He grabbed my hand and led me to the frozen seafood section, where we picked out some shrimp and mussels. Then we found bowtie pasta and alfredo sauce. As his contribution, he wanted French bread and a small bottle of olive oil.

We walked the rest of the way home as night crept in, both so electrified. Skipping half the way, we broke into song and cast euphoric glances to read each other's minds. It was more than giddy smiles and giggles; in this moment I felt like we were creating new universes and constellations. Children born tonight would live to love and smile often. We were not tangible in a real way; we were everything, nothing, and waiting at the beginning and the end of anything's existence. I felt, even though all we were doing was going home, we were doing something so important. More important than building cities or conquering mountains. More than converting heathens, creating babies, or winning the Olympics. We were so happy and so in love.

Bon worked secretively to beautifully wrap his gift to me. Using caution tape from a construction site, he tightly wrapped it, intentionally distorting the gift's shape. He found some shiny black feathers to decorate the top, and on Christmas Eve, both of our gifts were tucked under our tree.

I woke first on Christmas morning. Our house was quiet and cold. Snuggling in close to Bon, I let my mind wander and think of the beautiful secrets we kept between us. I knew this love that we shared was huge. At moments it seemed as though we would both burst. We were far too small to fit the entirety of that adult emotion inside our small frames. What could we do? It chose us, buried us, and we were happy to asphyxiate in it. In fifty years, would my heart still flutter when he says he loves me? I studied his profile in the dark and knew the answer—yes, even in a hundred years I would.

Bon stirred in his sleep, and I decided to warm our house before he had to kick off the blankets and start the day. I lit the candle and placed it far enough back on the shelf to shade the light from Bon's eyes. I found the Sterno stove, pot, and jug of water, preparing to make hot cocoa. I retrieved the cocoa powder from the shelf, along with two Halloween marshmallow and chocolate bats. We had been saving them for this morning, despite our teenage sweet tooth. As the water began to boil, I noticed Bon's breathing had changed. He was awake, waiting for me to wake him, and I felt a soft touch of mothering love compelling me. As I made up the two cups of cocoa, I sang softly, like my mother used to. I sat the cups on the board covering the entrance to the hut and sat down beside him. He tried not to smile as I leaned over to kiss his cheek, but I didn't let on that I knew.

"Wake up, honey. It's time to get up," I whispered while running my fingers through his hair.

He turned to cuddle into my knee sleepily, saying, "Merry Christmas, baby."

"Merry Christmas. If you make yourself vertical, you can have cocoa."

He gave a smile and wearily sat up. We set our chocolate and marshmallow bats to float in our cups and imagined at what the rest of the city was doing now. Halfway through our cocoa, the anticipation became too much. Bon knelt and reached, returning with the gifts. Handing me one, he insisted I go first. Unraveling the tape, I first came across a fine silver pen with a retractable tip, by far the nicest I had ever held. Under another layer of yellow tape was a writing book with our city depicted dreamily on the cover.

"A book to put all your stories in!" Bon excitedly told me. My expression must have given me away. "I just knew you would love it!" he added.

I was deeply touched; I loved it and realized at what depth my lover knew me, clear down to my soul.

"Thank you," I said, hugging him. "It's your turn."

I tore into the delicate wrapping to find a black box, but, oh, inside it. The one object that separated the boys from the men, nicer than my father's: a thick, black, leather wallet. Inside was a piece of inked paper that read, "To the boy of my heart as you become the man of my future."

It was the first adult gift I had ever received (save for socks and sweaters), and I was struck with a gorgeous sense of maturity. I'd always felt the impending inevitability of manhood, like being diagnosed with a disease and waiting for it to get worse. Maybe all this time I had been running away from home, I had really just been trying to outrun time. Now, all was different. With her patient love, I wanted to be a man. I always thought that growing up meant giving up on all my dreams. As Echo became partner in all my dreams, becoming a man became something to look forward to.

We finished our cocoa and wore away the morning listening to Azazel chirp Christmas carols. I made Echo my partner in filling the wallet, searching for anything that could make it seem essential. I took the small bills from savings, two fives and four ones. Our coffee shop punch card, Safeway club card, and a joker from my deck of playing cards that Echo had fashioned to look like a credit card. In the plastic photo sleeve, I placed a cut magazine picture of Einstein and told Echo we would have to get a camera.

When our restless youth could take no more, we went for a rainy walk. Simply amazed at the void of life on the streets, we imagined Santa Claus being really just a kingpin for a slave labor racket and the toys a way to launder money. We figured he kidnapped our neighbors in order to make next year's haul. We walked around the front of the grocery store, and I decided to call home; after all, it was Christmas. Echo seemed incredibly hesitant until I suggested she call her uncle. Calling collect, we told them how well we were doing and how much we were learning. They seemed calmed by the fact we had found one another and were not traveling alone, though my father sounded a little worried that my company was female. The usual persuasion to come home and the last "I love yous." We walked home a little quieter, lost in our own similar thoughts.

We saved our appetites for Christmas dinner, beginning preparations at around four o'clock. We worked together to prepare our feast. We drooled over the Sterno stove as the intoxicating smell of olive oil and shrimp filled the small enclosure.

We toasted and prayed to the god of love. We gorged ourselves on a very satisfying high-calorie meal, which incidentally lead to our early retirement.

Before the tourists with their thick wallets had come to Seattle, provisions were painfully low. We tried to hibernate, but when hunger had gotten so bad that not even a long-gone, stale cigarette could lend comfort, we had to adjust our concept of pride. Shame as we walked to the street we had long avoided. Weak with hunger, we joined the back of the line. Embarrassed, we held hands outside the soup kitchen. The line moved; we moved with it, but we tried to remain disconnected. Before we knew it, we were inside a fluorescent cafeteria of broken dreams.

"So many lonely faces," Echo whispered to the floor.

We were given a bowl of chicken broth and noodle soup with a dinner roll and found an empty gap at one of the long tables. We tried to eat, wishing we were invisible.

I think I saw him first, sitting as if in natural light, two sad faces to the right and across the table. A handsome man with bright, dazzling eyes. Sipping his soup with dignity, the elderly man looked as I imagined Jesus would have. His silver hair was groomed despite his worn clothing, which was itself not in bad repair. We looked to one another, Echo and I, feeling the same way. If he, with his integrity and pride, could sip soup here, so could we. We both sat a little straighter, inspired. For the first time this day, we fell into soft smiles. The flavor in the soup appeared as if we had only tasted our shame before. Hungrily we ate, soothing the aches in our stomachs and filling us with new life. As the man finished, he stood, cleared his Styrofoam bowl, and pushed in his chair. He took notice of us as he walked past, giving us a warm smile and bowing his head slightly. Echo and I were honored.

On our way home, we verbalized emotion and reaction concerning the soup kitchen incident. It felt oddly coincidental, as if a lesson had been taught, and life became easy again.

Time was changing, and we both knew it. The days were racing by quicker now, when they used to drag. Our eyes were broadening into the larger picture of the world, and we couldn't focus on pretend so easily anymore. This was both exciting and terrifying. What if we woke up tomorrow and realized we were old? We spent a few afternoons trying to be bored just to slow the time, being satisfied that we could if we wanted to. We marched on into the future. We had been together for a year now, on our own and surviving, but uncertainty would emerge just after Echo's fifteenth birthday.

Chapter 9

Spring had dressed our little forest, and we could once again come and go as we pleased. The tourists trickled in, and we had a set of ten songs rehearsed and pleasing enough to our listeners to put bread on our table.

One late afternoon as we neared home, we noticed a blue truck parked along our fence. As we drew closer, we saw two men surveying the property. Echo panicked.

"They're gonna find our house!"

"Hush, it'll be all right," I said, trying not to sound worried. "Let's just keep walking."

We walked around the neighborhood awhile, barking back at the dogs that barked at us, until the truck had gone. There, just outside the fence, was a four-foot-by-five-foot sign that had change for Echo and I written on it: "Coming Soon! Maple Family Apartments." We both felt the cold chill of eviction.

I woke the next morning to her gentle sobs. My dreary eyes found her packing. "Echo, baby," I soothed, touching her calf and struggling to my knees. She crouched in the small hut as she cleared the shelf.

"I don't wanna go. I like it here," she whimpered.

"I don't want to either." I spoke with remorse, putting my arms around her.

"Seems almost karmatic. I ran away from home; now my home keeps being taken from me." She attempted to transform solace into bitterness.

I helped her finish packing and tried to make her feel better, reminding her that home was wherever we were together. That night, I cradled her as we watched the sun set over Seattle for the last time.

Where to now? I wondered. *That way, I suppose.* We found ourselves sleeping in a park in Olympia. We used a car wash for a shower and a guitar for change, and life marched on.

After being in Olympia for almost a month, we found some kids—and I use the term kids very loosely. They were an interchangeable group of individuals ranging from thirteen to twenty-five years of age all oddly "marked" as belonging by dress and demeanor. Echo and I figured they were the "bad kids" that we weren't supposed to hang out with, but thus far they were the only type of people that would even associate with us. Were we bad? Dirty, yes, but I didn't see us as bad. Three of them, approximately our own age, invited us out to some secluded ruins of early industry that had thrived before it became cheaper to buy from China.

Echo and I were intrigued with the prospects of socialization, even if it was with bad people. We followed them across town, past the antiqued machine shops and auto garages, to a field of tall weeds. Gillian, Ben, and Courtney acquainted themselves with us while Bon and I acted as if we were all too accustomed to stranger company.

Through the weeds we were guided. Ahead I could see a dilapidated cement wall with remnants of wooden ceiling beams. Young trees grew up by the foundation, and ancient graffiti eroded along with the wall. On the narrow path we followed, there were rusty tin cans and shards of glass dispersed along the dusty, foot-printed trail. Upon our arrival I realized that this place was much larger than I had expected.

We entered what seemed to be a hallway or corridor to the left, with zombie graffiti and a few thick pipes rusting and staining the wall. To the right were doorways leading to rooms without roofs. One tall window led to a room with no door at all, just a few pipes and four windows, one in each wall. I was perplexed as to the structure's original function. A couple of the rooms had two walls in place of one: a single short, insulated wall with dirt against the other tall one; the two walls formed a shelf five feet from the ruble floor. The walls in the hallway sloped out at the bottom, giving them a comfortable, recliner effect, and so we sat. The rooms were full of cement chunks, aluminum cans, rocks, and broken bottles while the hall was nearly void of debris in comparison, with just a few large slabs of eroded cement and the earth. Wild things grew, as they do, out of cracks in the cement and over the ground in clusters.

"This might not be a bad place to stay," Echo noted as her eyes painted the ruins in colors only I knew she could create.

"Yeah, better than the park," I replied, noticing our company's interest.

"You guys runaways?" Ben asked with delicacy.

"Yes." Echo paused "Provided you're not a narc."

"We haven't anyone to tell anyhow," he reassured us, creating quiet.

"If our secret holds, you've got friends in us," I added to the sinking silence, reviving the atmosphere.

"I've always wanted to run away," Gillian said, "but never had a good excuse." Her words stung me unintentionally. I had no excuse to run, but I had anyway and found Echo. It was my destiny to meet her. When would I go home to right my wrongs? Suddenly shamed, I suppressed these thoughts.

Echo stretched her hands across the ground to our guitar case. She opened and lifted the guitar from where it rested, retrieving the disposable camera from the case's pick box. She asked if any of our company would take a few photos of the two of us. Courtney colorfully agreed, stood, and claimed the camera.

We had purchased the camera a few days ago, using a few shots to take portraits of one another, but we longed to have pictures of us together.

We indulged Courtney's instigated poses, so long as it remained true to our wondering selves. She had us sit on top of one of the walls and aimed the camera so our backdrop was the gray sky. Standing, holding hands against a wall of graffiti, and kissing.

We followed Courtney to a toppled smokestack that had left much rubble and a deep hole in the ground. As we drew to the far side, I noticed a long parallel tunnel jutting from the base of the bricked hole. The jagged circumference was approximately twenty feet. I brought up the tail as we descended to the dirt floor seven feet below.

Courtney suggested we pose in the tunnel's entrance. Echo and I took opposite walls, leaned our backs against them, and held hands. We smiled at each other, not the camera.

Courtney returned the camera, received our thanks, and encouraged us to explore the tunnel. She said it went back at least one hundred feet, getting smaller as it went, but that there was a narrow exit on the other side that was almost impossible to notice.

"It's nice and dry in here," Echo relayed as she made her way deeper into the tunnel. The walls were rocky, and the ground was made of soft, dry sand and silt. I fallowed Echo, with Courtney behind me.

"It's a cool place to chill when the rain won't let up," Courtney informed us.

The ground made its way closer to the ceiling, and before long we were crawling in total blackness. Echo described a dim light, crawled a ways farther, and then disappeared. In her stead I could see filtered light coming from a small rocky opening. I followed suit, squeezing and wiggling out of the ground to find myself emerging under a rather large bush.

"That is too cool!" Echo exclaimed "I guess it's no wonder where we're sleeping tonight."

I nodded my head in agreement, waiting for Courtney to surface.

"Uh, you guys, I think I'm stuck," an embarrassed voice resonated from under the bush.

Echo and I grinned, laughing under our breath before returning to help her get out.

"Ever since puberty, I've felt like a cat with trimmed whiskers. I'm not quite comfortable in this body yet," Courtney said, swiping the dirt from her light blue jeans and gray hoodie.

I could see the affinity in Echo's eyes as she smiled at Courtney, but she said nothing.

We walked around the ruins to rejoin Gillian and Ben, who were by then spray painting on one of the blank walls.

"Pick a color," Gillian invited, pointing to a light-blue backpack leaning against the adjacent wall. She was working on an orange abstract flower, while Ben was writing his first name in large blue letters.

Echo didn't hesitate; she went to the bag and retrieved a can of green paint. Setting to work on a large circle behind Gillian, she experimented with the can to familiarize herself with it.

"It's gonna be a planet," she told me as she turned to get another color. Inspired, I busied myself trying to find a piece of cardboard in order to make a star stencil. It didn't take long to find an abandoned thirty-pack beer box. It was empty and a little weathered, but it would suit my purpose just fine. I pulled the box's seams apart, laid it flat, and cut a couple different star shapes, leaving them spaced to avoid over spray. When the stencils were complete, Echo was finishing the blue rings around her four-foot planet.

"Now for a red one," she said to me as she returned to the blue backpack. She handed me the silver and black paint and grabbed the cherry red for herself.

The group painted and without words forged an accessory alliance. We were bad kids now, but it felt good, exciting but more comfortable then I would have thought. I could tell Echo felt the same; we were a misfit army of outcast youth subconsciously bound together. Who could say for what real reason, but I figured it was because we rejected the PC concepts of happiness and lifestyle. We liked to live in our heads; we were free thinkers with our perceptions a little obscured.

They passed a few lit cigarettes around, including Echo and I in the rotation. I viewed tobacco as a medicine useful in taking the bite off hunger but found it silly to abuse it outside its attributes. Echo and I longed for acceptance, so we pretended before passing it to the next person.

When dusk lay impending on the horizon, the kids said their good-byes and made promises to see us the next day. They were concerned about our comfort, but we assured them we would sleep well. Echo and I watched them disappear across the field.

We ate noodles for dinner and slept soundly, curled up together in the depths of the tunnel.

Echo and I admired our unfinished mural in the rare, uninhibited morning sun before giving ourselves a tour of the surrounding property. The vast area came up behind a car wash and an auto garage. On the other side was a steep hill with a few old houses on it. The ruins were barely visible from the property's outskirts due to the vegetation. All and all a good place to squat for a while.

We would meet several new people over the next couple of months. The ruins were a beacon for the abnormal who always congregated in the afternoons to be bad. We gained a strange and appealing new perspective of life as wispy and worthless. With the flood of social situations came the inevitable bad influences. Echo and I, with our thirst for experience, gave in hesitantly, cautiously, and, as always, together.

Gillian, Ben, and Courtney were already there when we returned home from a full day of panhandling and a trip to the grocery store. They wore soft, vacant smiles like I had never seen before. A few of the other usual suspects were there, crowding around a black duffle bag. The sky was gray, and the remaining light in it was long past lent and now failing. They gave us a warm homecoming, as though we had been gone for years. Echo and I exchanged confused glances.

Ben stood up, spoke softly to one of the older boys, and with his consent pulled two shiny cans from the black bag.

"Ta-da," Ben enthused, walking the cans to us.

"Thanks." I naturally replied before inspecting the can he had pushed into my hand. Cheap beer. I looked to Echo, whose face was in a state of awkward panic. She held her can with her bent elbow against her side, extending it away from herself. I spared a goofy grin to settle her, moving to sit by a rusty pipe with the others in the cement hallway. I led her by the hand to sit on the other side of the pipe that protruded only an inch and a half from the cement. As I placed our grocery sack between us, I slid my beer into the pipe. Ever so quietly, I told Echo to open hers. As she did, she looked as though the crack of the seal would summon her parents. With another smile from me, she took a sip, pulled her knees in closer to her chest, and then took another. She set the beer between us in front of the grocery bag and gave me a devious smirk.

We shared the beer slowly, being cautious not to allude to so much. Both times Ben returned to the duffle bag to get himself another, he grabbed us a couple too, which we fed to the pipe. In the dark, Echo and I pretended to be drunk (not a difficult undertaking, considering we were already weird), laughing and carrying on like our friends. We turned down the last round and drank from an empty can. As their energy peaked, so did ours. In the starless night, dark as guilty eyes, we sang, dreamed, and joked. Courtney and Gillian began to whine about a lack of toilet paper. Echo, like the skilled adventurer she was, pulled a wad from her back pocket. The girls, as they always do, went in a group behind the ruin's outer wall. Ben joked about trying to scare the girls into falling into their own puddles, but as gentlemen do, he laughed and stayed put.

The girls returned some time later, Gillian complaining of an ill stomach. There were whispers of wanting a tooth brush and a strategy to hide Gillian's jacket from her parents. The group dispersed with happy, slurred good-byes, and Echo and I were left to our own devices. We fished the five cans from the pipe and brought them back to the tunnel, saving them for a braver day.

Gifts became common; canned food and leftovers made panhandling more sport than survival. The gifts freed up our time, so we spent most of it with friends. On occasion, Echo and I scheduled a night where we both slept over at a friend's house. We enjoyed the opportunity to shower, receive a decent meal, and even have adult supervision—or rather, their caring presence. I became rather skilled at video games and knowledgeable about late-night television. Echo, on the other hand, seemed to know everything about everyone. Echo and I always missed each other terribly around midnight. When we reunited the next day, we couldn't stop wanting to kiss.

One afternoon, while Echo and I were playing hangman in the hallway, we heard charismatic laughter from along the trail. We followed the sound, discreetly investigating, bearing witness to a most generous commotion. Gillian and Ben were fumbling with a twin-size mattress and clumsily navigating the brush. Touched in a deep way, we lost ourselves in their thoughtfulness before regaining our senses to run and help them. A grinning Gillian announced it was a present, and they gladly shared with us the happy burden.

With quite a bit of effort, we pulled and pushed the mattress down the tunnel, till it would go no further. It bowed in a slight U shape against the walls, insuring that in the nights to come, we would be drawn together by gravity as we slept.

"Can you believe we found it in the alley behind the furniture store? It's practically new!" Gillian volunteered as she followed Echo to crouch-walk out of the tunnel.

We slept so soundly night after night, wrapped within each other's arms, the heart of the planet pulling us together.

We woke feeling brave. The early morning sky was clear, and company had yet to find us. We took Azazel and the reserved "minor possession" to the far side of the property and hid within a fortress of bushes. Each taking up a can, we cracked them and toasted to love. The beer was warm, altering its already strangely gross flavor. It made us burp a lot but didn't have any altering effects till we had each put away half a can. Slowly, we began to giggle about nothing, feeling our stomachs go warm. We described the sensations to one another as I kept an eye on the time. An hour, one beer apiece, and we were dizzy, silly, and astonishingly stupid. Not yet slurring, just not making all the neurological connections. It was fun. We opened the next round, the flavor a bit more palatable than before. The world's colors seemed a little strange now, like we were looking through screened photo lenses. Echo laughed like crazy people do when they talk to themselves, and I fell into it with her. Another hour, our beers were empty, leaving us one to share.

"Let's go exploring," Echo excitedly suggested, barely able to keep herself settled. Feeling restless, I agreed. We left our shelter and wandered the far side of the property. We found a gap in the bottom of the fence behind the auto garage. Sliding along the ground to make it under the fence, Echo's belt loop became caught on the chain link, and we giggled as we fumbled to set her free. We walked around close to home, being sure not to draw attention while Echo collected pretty bottle caps.

Within an hour and a half, the effects were fading, so we searched out a place to split the last warm beer. A tree grew along an alleyway, its thick branches heavy with millions of leaves. With the beer in my pocket, I ascended the tall tree, Echo coming up close behind. We found a covered, thick limb and sat on it, taking care to make ourselves comfortable. As I retrieved the snugly tucked can from my pocket I fumbled. The beer fell from the tree and hit the asphalt with a bounce. Starting softly, Echo tittered, her laugh becoming more absurd. Echo's laughter became all, and my repose was lost. Hushing her giggles between my own, I climbed back down to retrieve the well-shaken beer. I conquered the tree once more. We waited some time, Echo gently tapping the lid of the can as I clutched it firmly in my right hand. We drank the strange water, left the can hanging in the tree, and continued on our walk.

We returned to our home, crawled under the fence, and went to the bushes to retrieve Azazel.

"We're bad parents," Echo announced with a sigh.

"What do you mean?" I inquired, peering over her shoulder.

She flipped the power switch. "We left him on while we were gone. Now the batteries are dead," Echo mourned.

"Maybe we should get a babysitter the next time we go on a bender," I teased.

"I think you're right." She collapsed the antenna, and we left in laughter.

Returning to the ruins, we noticed someone we had not seen before. He wasn't one of us—an older man, early forties, slightly shorter than average, wearing blue jeans and a jeans jacket. He hadn't seen us yet, so we remained concealed, gazing through the foliage of tall weeds and young trees.

Though the beer had worn off, we still had the giggles. Hiding our presence, we covered our mouths to keep from laughing out loud. It felt so silly to hide from a lone adult—on our turf, nonetheless. The man had black hair—brown-black, not blue-black—and it was wavy. He wore a mullet cut and a pair of glasses. On one sleeve of his jeans jacket there were colored patches, but we were too distant to make them out. The back was painted with an abstract design that reminded me of a tire track and road kill. He was retrieving thick markers from a little blue bucket and drawing around one of the window sills.

The man's diligent hands worked softly on the cement. His contented eyes shined in his passion and play. I can't explain it; he held himself in a shifty, happy sort of way, a little goofy maybe. I didn't know a single thing about him, but I liked him. He reminded me of my uncle a little, maybe my dad.

In the distance I could hear Gillian and Ben bickering as they drew near to the ruins. The man must have heard them too, because he returned his markers to the blue pail, picked it up, and circled the outer side of the structure. He waited till Ben and Gillian had entered the ruin's hallway, and then slipped away down the dirt path. I don't know why I cared, but I did. The stranger seemed lonely, and it made me sad.

We would see the man every once in a while, but we always let him alone, keeping ourselves like shadows so as not to scare him away. His paint pen art was like nothing I had seen before, uniquely abstract and meticulously flawless. Bon and I began leaving compliments in magic marker below his pieces as a way to encourage his return. We started referring to him as "Dad" because we didn't know his name.

Chapter 10

One late afternoon, while Bon and I were reading, Gillian showed up to the tunnel toting a full backpack and a bed roll.

"Echo, my mom said I could spend the night at your house," she exclaimed with a disbelieving expression. "You've been over to my house several times, and my mom likes you. My folks are going out tonight, so here I am."

Bon used a blade of dry straw as a bookmark and we stood up.

"Of course she doesn't know you live in a tunnel out at the factory ruins, but she didn't ask." Gillian was excited, this being the closest thing to running away she herself could condone.

I had never been hostess for a sleepover, and the idea thrilled me. Bon read the situation and volunteered his departure, claiming he would like the opportunity to beat one of Ben's video games. Bon kissed me, told me to be careful, and then departed.

I was responsible for showing Gillian what it was like to be an irresponsible wreck. Honored, I pondered what aspects I should show her. I figured the half bag of tortillas Bon and I had planned on eating for dinner wouldn't suffice for a guest. I would take Gillian out to panhandle, and we could get something to go with them.

Gillian followed me into the tunnel. Setting her bag on the mattress, I searched in the dark for the guitar, retrieved it, and we set out.

"I brought money," Gillian said.

I brushed off the comment, stating, "It tastes better when you work for it." She smiled, understanding what I meant.

We took turns with the guitar, singing in a drizzle outside of the grocery store. Most people tried to ignore us, so I began to get a little more aggressive, asking for pocket change. Gillian would blush slightly when someone would drop money in the guitar case, and it made me remember how embarrassed I used to get. Within forty-five minutes, we had made enough scratch to get a small block of cheddar and a single-serving tub of salsa. Quesadillas it would be. Gillian seemed proud of the meager haul.

We cooked on the Sterno stove outside in the last glow of sunlight and then retreated into the tunnel and ate in candle shadows. After dinner I told stories of Bon's and my adventures, and we shared cigarettes. Then she asked a question that stumped me.

"Are you and Bon a sexual couple?"

I didn't know if I should tell the truth or if I should lie. She was my age, wasn't she? Bon and I had always been so overwhelmed in kisses that I hadn't thought about pushing it further.

"Well, no," I finally answered.

"Sorry, I just couldn't imagine you guys sleeping next to each other all the time and nothing ever happening." Gillian giggled, embarrassed.

"We've always slept next to each other, since we were strangers. I still get dizzy when he kisses me; I think if he went up my shirt I'd have a heart attack." I smiled at the honesty in my statement.

Gillian laughed. "He's never touched your boob?" She gasped between outbursts of amusement. "I haven't had sex yet, but I've been groped before."

I suddenly felt self-conscious.

"I am curious, though. About sex, not your modesty," Gillian laughed.

We spoke in whispers about boys and sex. Only then did I wonder if Bon liked me in that way. I knew he loved me, but did he love me in a procreation sort of way? Should I care yet? Gillian and I agreed by the end of the conversation that we were in no hurry to grow up.

Gillian had a hard time falling asleep, but she found solace when I told her that I was sure Bon would drag Ben out at first light to check on us. By now, I knew Bon as well as I knew myself. As I predicted, they were there when I woke, with hot cups of coffee and smiles.

"You girls have fun?" Bon inquired, finding my hand to hold in the dark shadows. I smiled at his soft silhouette in the distant light filtering in from tunnel's mouth. I admitted I missed him more than fun could have comforted me, and there in the belly we whispered and sipped coffee as we waited for Gillian to wake up.

Gillian was part Chinese, with dark—to medium-brown hair and eyes to match. She was smart and funny, and when she was around, I felt a little braver. I liked staying at her house better than staying at Courtney's for the company and cuisine. Gillian was always engaging, insightful, and educational, and her mother cooked the most amazing food I had ever tasted. Gillian thought she was fat, but that's only because she couldn't see through my eyes. She wore glasses. She wore skirts a lot, really long ones of all different colors, and a few she made. She looked like a punk-hippie crossbreed, with her short spiked hair and flip flops.

In the following months, Bon and I took to stealing, not by urge to but out of lack of better options. We had brought in our disposable camera to be developed and must have miscalculated the prints' cost. We hadn't sufficient funds to pay for them and, unwilling to endure an uncertain wait, we stole. I didn't try to hide them; we simply walked out of the store. Holding his hand in my right and cradling the envelope of photos against my side, we just walked out. Just like that. It was so easy we couldn't help it, and it took less time than begging. We kept our sticky fingers for occasional items, expensive ones like a white plastic bottle of multivitamins and batteries for Azazel. We indulged our shame in stealing in order to conceal our fear of getting caught. It was hard to keep my composure, though, when Bon was forced to walk with a seemingly dead leg to keep the bottle of vitamins from rattling in his pocket as we passed by the cash register.

We affectionately called him Dad, the shy graffiti artist with the soft eyes. Elusive as he was, Bon and I made a game of hiding and trying to catch him painting with his markers. One morning we woke to find a care package just outside the tunnel entrance. In a plain cardboard box signed with a line drawing on a note card was treasure. Two bright-green apples, two big oranges, a six pack of grape soda, and a bag of Jolly Ranchers. There was also a bag of Doritos, a box of cookies, and a huge French-bread sandwich. Bon and I were overwhelmed, warm, and cared for; in our minds, he truly became our dad.

We fashioned a thick thank you card from a piece of the cardboard box. Borrowing paint from Gillian, we decorated it and taped it to his latest graffiti.

He continued to bring us gifts every other week. After school started for our friends, we came to rely on his generosity, leaving him bottle cap mosaics and short stories in return. Four months would pass before we tried to approach him. It was lightly drizzling rain, and he was continuing his work on the eastern outside wall. Bon and I slowly approached him. He wore a nervous grin, finished his line, and then smiled at us.

"What do ya think?" he said, taking a step back and admiring his work.

"It's beautiful," I admitted, moving a little closer to him, Bon by my side. The pen painting looked like an abstract tree aflame or dressed for fall.

"Brilliant color play," Bon complimented, stepping in close to the wall to inspect the piece.

"Thanks for all the food," I said feeling my cheeks turn hot with embarrassment.

"No problem." Dad smiled. My flushed cheeks abated when I noticed his right hand fiddling with the red paint pen he held. It seemed as though he was trying to use the little mixing ball inside the metal casing to calm his own nerves.

Bon moved in closer to me, brushing his hand across my forearm and smiling in his confidence. "My name is Bon, and this is my love, Echo." He beamed and held out his hand.

The man pocketed the paint pen and took up Bon's traditional greeting. "Roy," he replied with an awkward grace. The skin around his eyes gave his age away, probably mid-forties, but in them he looked like a boy who was not yet a man.

"How long have you kids been living down here?" Roy asked with loving eyes.

"For the summer," Bon answered.

"Are you kids from around here?"

Bon and I said nothing, fearing what information could be used to send us home.

"I'm not going to divulge to anyone, just making conversation." He was looking a little scolded.

"I'm from Colorado," I said smiling.

"Arizona," Bon said.

Roy smiled. "Long way from home. You kids adventurers?"

"Yeah," Bon and I remarked in unison, our confidence restored.

"Well . . . I've got a workshop just a little up the road, and it's equipped with a small one-room apartment above it. I've got a house on the other side of town; I bought the workshop for fun, so the apartment is useless to me. You could live there for as long as you want." Dad stumbled over his words, seemingly terrified of being declined. Maybe he was simply scared of how it might come across, a grown man luring two runaways home. I smiled at his sincerity and thought it sad that generosity had to hide because of its potential to be abused.

Bon could not resist. "So long as we can call you Dad," he said half-jokingly.

Roy smiled and his eyes shined. "That's all right with me." He pulled a set of keys from his pocket. "The big one is for the gate, and the smaller one is for the apartment. It's just over the hill on the main road to the left. I'd like to help you move, but I've got to get home. You'll be all right. You can't miss it."

Roy gathered his paint pens, bid us farewell, and headed out across the field.

Bon looked to me, excitement swelling inside him and being forced out of his wide smile. "We have an apartment!"

The rest of the day we spent packing. When school let out, Gillian and Ben helped us move everything except the mattress up the hill. Roy had been right—the place was hard to miss. Atop the hill began a fence, tall, chain-linked, and long. Approximately fifty feet from where it started was a driveway gate of plain-looking metal pipe and chain link. On the simple latch was a rather large padlock, and the key fit effortlessly into the riddled slot. With a quarter turn, it popped and unlocked. My stomach fluttered with excitement. We entered the weedy, dirt driveway, taking in the large yard. A metal real estate sign lay to the right of the fence, and car parts, appliances, and roofing shingles were scattered across the property. There were over two acres of junk. Not far to the right of the fence's gate stood the property's only permanent structure, a large garage with two fifteen-foot bay doors that would swing out on massive hinges. Along the left side was a smaller door intended for foot traffic.

We walked to the back of the garage and mounted the spiraling stair case. There was a window in the garage's wall just at the base of the steps. I peered in but could see nothing in the gloomy interior. The apartment was built above the garage; a small deck with wooden railing and two weathered white metal chairs greeted us as we reached the landing. Two windows with yellow cloth curtains and the door looked out over the cluttered yard. The structure was stucco and painted a light tan—no contrasting trim, just tan. It had been recently painted, but I could tell where the previous layers had chipped and disappeared.

Bon set his bag in one of the chairs and moved to unlock the door.

"This place is so cool," Gillian said, shuffling in her anticipation to enter the apartment. I couldn't tell if she was excited to see the interior or simply put down the large box she carried. Perhaps both.

The door swung to the outside, and we entered. Inside, the air was dusty but soft. Shadows were birthed from the glowing light soaking in from the only two windows. Ben flicked on the only light, a single bulb in the ceiling. The shadows recoiled to reveal the largest enclosed dwelling Bon and I had ever shared. The floor was carpeted in brown shag, and the walls were textured white. To the right of the door was a humble counter with blue tiles and a wooden cupboard beneath it. Next to it was a tiny stove with an oven that looked almost like a toy. A green refrigerator with plain circular magnets and an empty book shelf brought up the right side to the back wall.

To the left side, only four feet across from the oven, a futon had been pushed against the wall. A folded blue blanket and two white pillows lay on the black mattress. Beyond the bed's silver metal frame was a homemade end table constructed out of four weathered and squared wooden posts with a rectangular particleboard top. Decorative cast iron angles held the pieces together, and atop the table was a wide white candle. Beyond the table was a bit of open floor space before reaching the back wall and presumably the bathroom door.

We set all our belongings on the floor beside the end table. I went to open the bathroom door and find the light switch. A ball-link chain only four inches long descended from the mounted wall fixture, and the frosted glass softened the bulb's light.

In front of the door was the only sink in the apartment, antiqued porcelain atop a decorative pedestal with a book-sized mirror mounted to the wall above it. To the left was a small, plain, white tiled shower with an oversized purple shower curtain. The drain had a little rust around its edges. Along the inside wall was a metal towel rack with two new white towels hanging from it. Behind the door, against the far right wall, was the toilet. Above it was a built-in cupboard with three shelves and a package of toilet paper. The bathroom was very small—only four feet from the doorway to the mirror above the sink. It was wider, though, and big enough to fit three people with no elbow room.

Bon and I felt almost like we were in our own fairytale. Not believing our luck, we kept exchanging kisses, intent on waking each other in case we were only dreaming. Overcome with euphoria and gratitude, we cheerfully put away our meager possessions.

Ben and Gillian stayed a few hours to admire the apartment and envy us. We made plans to have sleepovers and chill parties, but nothing that might get us in trouble with Roy. Bon and I knew that keeping a low profile would be essential for keeping the apartment, but expecting us not to have a few small get-togethers would be too much. Our company departed as dinner bells rang, and the two of us felt our own insistent stomachs.

Bon filled our little pot with water from the bathroom sink and put it on the electric burner. I made up our bed, electing not to possession it flat for fear their wouldn't be enough room on the floor. We were small enough to both fit comfortably with it positioned like a couch anyway.

While waiting for the water to boil, Bon sat next to me on the couch. My stomach fluttered. He still did that to me, even after so long, and I wondered when I would become immune. I hoped I never did. I wanted that boy to cause the heart attack that killed me when we're a hundred and ten. He leaned over to kiss my earlobe.

We made spaghetti and play fought over who got to use the fork (the other had gone MIA over a week before). Play fighting with Bon was more fun than with Mr. Bear, although I did miss that silly stuffed animal who could only stare back at me with his sad, plastic eyes. I relented this time when Bon purposed we eat from the pot and he would feed me every other bite.

Azazel cooed as Bon and I laid on the futon, cuddling. Our minds were racing in the dark. We shared our excitement and speculated about what the future might hold for us now. We were blessed, truly. Bon and I felt an awesome wash of gratitude, thanking the universe for making Roy the wonderful person that he was. Every perfect day and every hardship our dad had survived in his past made him the person we admired tonight. We just wished that there was something that we could do to make his life as beautiful as he has made ours. Pondering on this debt to repay, we fell quiet but didn't sleep.

I couldn't keep my eyes closed. I just had to look into the dark of our first real apartment. Every time, the vague sight made my stomach flutter. I tried to sleep but became aware of the sun rising just outside the windows. I gave up and decided to watch Bon for a while.

His soft eyelids fluttered and lifted to reveal those dark brown eyes laced in black lashes. He smiled, scoffed, and rolled his eyes.

"Yeah, I know, me too," he whispered. He kissed my nose and then suggested we get up.

We untangled ourselves and set to work preparing for the day. There was water to boil for hot black coffee over shared smiles of excitement.

"Let's clean up the yard," I suggested. "We could surprise him."

Bon smiled at me over his glasses. "That's a good idea. Maybe with enough manual labor, we can fall asleep."

We didn't bother with showers before setting to work. My stomach went all summersaults as my hand clutched the doorknob. It was the door to our first place—ours. I stepped out to our deck and looked out over the shabby yard.

"My stomach's got butterflies," Bon said, closing the door behind him.

He was just as excited as I was, and caught in a perfect moment, I turned around. I wrapped my arms around his neck, and we kissed for the entire world to see. Young, lucky, and in love—could life get any better? It felt as though if I was any happier, I would burst.

It took much effort to give the kiss an end, but eventually we did. Shivering in the morning cool, we descended the stairs, eager to warm ourselves with work. Not sure where to start and overwhelmed with endless work, we were up to the challenge.

"Let's start in the front and work our way back," Bon said, leading me by the hand around the building. We observed the damage and made a game plan. We needed five piles: glass, scrap metal, paper/organic, plastic, and one for the unavoidable landfill material. We would burn the paper and plant matter then recycle what we could. Bon found a small lidless charcoal barbeque grill and set it at the unclear boundary where the driveway met the yard.

"We'll make the piles next to the grill," Bon noted and we began gathering the debris. Beer bottles, candy wrappers, graded homework from some kid named John, rusty engine parts, a fender, and all those roofing shingles. I found a manual weed whacker, and after we had cleared the trash from the front yard and the length of the fence, Bon lit the fire and I began leveling the weeds.

We received a lot of smiles from neighbors driving past in their vehicles, so we knew it was looking better. Bon gathered the severed weeds and fed them to the smoky fire, and by late afternoon, the front yard was cleared. The overgrown evergreen attempt at hedges along the drive were trimmed by Bon with a pair of rusty scissors. The hearty green spears nearly refused to burn as I slowly fed them to the fire. Similar evergreen bushes grew sparsely by the fence, and we did our best to make them presentable.

Hungry and tired, we abandoned the recyclables for tomorrow and went upstairs for showers, ramen noodles, and a nap. Ah, sleep.

We woke in time to make coffee and nestle in our chairs out on the deck. Sipping hot, instant coffee, we watched the sunset in pink and orange, satisfied. My heart felt fluttery and good, and my muscles ached a little. I felt so grown up, responsible, elegant even, and as usual, in love. We shared smiles as I watched the colors change on the lenses of his glasses. As he spoke of future plans for the apartment, the rest of our lives played out in my mind. Destiny had wrapped us together. There was no denying we were gonna last forever. Innocent as your first kiss, we were eternal.

Chapter 11

The next day, when the sun was warm, Bon and I were equipped for the task at hand. We had discovered a wagon amongst the property's infinite junk. The wagon was rusty and had a hole through the bottom the size of a quarter. Once we had done our best to straighten the rear axle, we loaded the recyclables and tied them down.

Our first stop was at the grocery store to unload the plastic bottles and glass into their appropriate receptacles. The wagon was barely any lighter when we were done, so we toiled on clear across town to the metal scrap yard. What interesting expressions people had as we made our way. Bon and I made faces back or smiled and waved. The man at the scrap yard paid us four dollars and sixty cents for our junk. We took the wagon up hills so we could ride it back down on our way home.

We wouldn't see Roy for another two days, but when we did, the expression on his face said more than any dictionary. His eyes misted like he might cry, and he had a smile that dominated his cheeks. Bon and I knew our hard work had repaid in part our debt of kindness.

We had been exploring the weeded junk spread over the back field when Roy's white truck had pulled into the drive. Like children do when daddy comes home, we ran to meet him.

"You guys didn't have to do all this." Dad smiled as we jogged the remaining ten feet.

"We just really appreciate all you've done for us. It's the least we could do," Bon replied, wiping his dirty hands on his light-blue jeans.

"Well, thank you."

"Our pleasure." I smiled.

"You kids wanna see my workshop?"

We nodded and followed him to the side door. He unlocked it with his modest set of keys. It was dark and chilled inside. I lost Roy as he presumably went to turn on the light. There was a clatter and swear words disguised with clumsy laughter. Then the large doors parted one at a time as he pushed them open. Light flooded in and oh, what strange wonders.

A Guinness beer light hung on the wall just to the right of the door. My eyes followed the sign's electrical cord to a battered green couch. The cushions and arm rests were filthy but accompanied the room like a cousin. To the right of the couch was another home-crafted end table with a gray clay bowl full of individually wrapped candies. A wooden coffee table courageously stood before the couch with stacks of magazines underneath it—Playboys, Maxims, and, to my astonishment, a small stack of five books of poetry by Rod McKuen. Atop the table was a cup of markers, pens, and pencils, and a sketch book. To the left was a set of three five-foot tall lockers of knitted steel with a stereo inside.

To the left of the door was a large plastic sink stained with paints, wood stains, and numerous other substances. The window under the stairs was visible from where I stood; I could hardly see out of it, it was so filthy. To the right of the window against the rear wall was a little room with a closed door. A poster of a Budweiser girl decorated the plain white paint just above the round knob. The far wall was decorated with silk plants, flowers, and a four-foot tree in a plastic pot. Black plastic netting stuck out from the edges of the green silk carpet on the wall. It was beautiful, a man's secret Eden not quite complete. Bon and I admired it a while. A professional drafting table had been meticulously placed in the middle of the room on a red scrap of short carpet (the floor was otherwise cement). If you sat down to draw, the bathroom would be behind you, the open bay doors behind your work, couch to your right, and Eden to the left. Shelves, jars of hardware, empty frames, cans of paint, a dresser, and much more random debris in the garage would soak in for months to come.

Roy picked up the blue pail of paint markers he had previously sent crashing to the floor from an upside-down milk crate.

"Have a seat, if you want," he invited correcting the crate and replacing the pail.

Bon and I flopped down on the couch to admire Dad's hide out, giving thought to how we would like to be when we grew up—just like Dad. He sat next to Bon and began to tell us about himself, throwing his feet on the coffee table and sinking into the cushions.

Dad worked as an engineer in a large machinery factory. His work bored him but afforded him the opportunity to do the things he was more passionate about: art, thought, and architecture. He liked to design earth-friendly houses and business buildings, and he was currently working on a chapel. He sometimes wrote poetry when he felt moved to do so, and he loved philosophy, religious ideals, and evolution. Dad loved his world. The reality we all knew was somehow obscured as it passed into his awareness. Life was a beautiful thing; everyone had their redeeming qualities. As he spoke I felt strangely compelled to protect him and his ideals.

Dad led us around the shop, explaining what everything was for. He showed us his house and building blue prints, let us look through a professional black box of his artwork, and even allowed us to take one to hang on the wall of the apartment. A signature Roy piece, Bon and I agreed. It had two large circles interlocked by colored line layers and accentuated with sharp lines through them that never touched. Roy gave us a blue tack, and we were excitedly grateful to have a Roy original.

Dad took us out for pizza then dropped us off at the apartment. Bon and I felt almost religious in an awesome way; without a thing to offer, we were loved.

A tinge of guilt came as we circled up the stairs in the last light of sundown.

"Do you suppose he planned to get something accomplished today?" Bon inquired.

We had selfishly eaten up all his time, but bedding suspicion, I said, "Nah, he did most of the talking." Bon reached the landing. "It was us that couldn't get away."

Bon smiled at me. "Yeah, but let's make sure we don't wear out our welcome."

I agreed, and we entered the apartment. Tomorrow would be a big day; we were low on provisions and had to go play downtown to resupply. We went to bed early, stuffed with pizza and soda.

Echo was a woman, no longer a child, and I had only suddenly realized it. I knocked on the back door because I had locked myself out, and Echo rushed in nothing more than a towel to let me in. She was soft, her hair was wet, and she was covered in smiles. Her boyish figure had turned to curves overnight it seemed. Perhaps her baggy clothes simply kept them from me. I tried not to stare as she picked out new clothes, but I allowed myself a glimpse as she returned to the bathroom to change. I had to focus on something else.

We made the apartment out to fit us, collaborating on decoration. We hung circuit boards from random appliances on the walls, leaving wires to dangle. A few collages were stuck together with toothpaste, and we put a picture of us on the refrigerator. Cliché sayings were written in strange locations: "Haste makes waste" on the toilet tank, "A rolling stone gathers no moss" on the top landing of the stairs. We took a hubcap and made paper arms like a clock to glue to it. We set the "clock" to one forty; no reason, it just looked like a plausible position.

Roy found us honest work. He told us we would be working for the Carriage Hotel and Diner doing odd jobs, cleaning rooms, helping in the diner, whatever Larry the hotel's owner needed. Colder, wetter months were approaching, which always made it harder to live out of the pockets of strangers. Bon and I were scared we might get caught stealing, so the opportunity of employment seemed heaven sent. Roy and Larry were friends. Roy didn't want us stealing anymore, and Larry needed laborers he could pay less and under the table, so they got together and formulated our employment. We were grateful.

Our first day of work was Monday at six in the morning. We were ecstatic and scared and so proud. We weren't taxpayers, but it was honest. Dad bought us a battery-powered alarm clock to insure we would not be late our first day.

The hotel was old, one of the first built in Olympia. The diner was very small, and the menu was minimal, consisting of sandwiches, soup and salads, hamburgers, fries, and so on. The lobby was small but furnished, and Larry stood behind the front desk, which looked more like a bar. He was around the same age as Dad but looked older somehow.

Larry greeted us with a firm handshake that nearly crushed my hand, and his gray eyes smiled instead of his mouth. He seemed a little timid. Taking us on could be a bad decision if he got caught. I assured him it was important to conceal our employment. He relaxed and walked us around the entire hotel.

The rooms were small, each one unique and decorated to match how the hotel would have been originally furnished. There was the cleaning supply room, the laundry room, and even an employee lounge with the time clock and a microwave. Larry promised us we could eat one free meal in the diner a day (due to our cheap labor) and that if we ever wanted to stay in one of the rooms, it would be half off. For today he set us up cleaning rooms and doing laundry with a lady named Maggie, who was a little crazy, and said that tomorrow he would put us in the diner.

We cleaned rooms, checked people in and out of the hotel, and worked the small diner. I'd cook while Echo waited tables. We could afford to stop stealing, and much of the city smiled to see the two of us with real jobs.

We played guitar in the small earth-toned lobby for fun when business was slow. Echo wrote some short stories and left them in drawers of our more frequently used rooms. She included a blank page for comments, but more often than not, her stories were swiped. Echo felt honored.

We worked hard and quickly grew on our boss, who began to feed us twice a day and allow us all the free coffee we could drink. We were rich. I even saved up and paid my uncle back. Not just the money—I wrote him a rude letter as well. Roy helped Echo and I get a post office box in Seattle. We checked it once a month when we could get a ride. Echo kept in close contact with her uncle; I sent letters to my family but didn't feel safe giving them the PO box. I told them all about Echo, figuring they would come to the wedding someday and should know a little about her. It was funny because in my letters I wrote as though I was away at summer camp, neglecting to mention that I had been gone for almost two years. Strange. Echo also began to write to Kelly in Chicago.

As Christmas approached, my guilt weighed on me. I missed my dad. Echo knew; I couldn't keep even my thoughts from her. She suggested I send them the PO box address. *Not yet,* I thought. *A few nights more. I can't tell her out loud what I've done.* I was scared Echo wouldn't understand. Maybe she would hate me for running a way for "fun." *A few more nights.*

Echo did all she could to cheer me up at work. She made me snowflakes from the coffee filters, made my lunch for me, and kept smiles waiting. I did my best, but the Christmas decorations and happy families were a relentless reminder.

We talked after a few days, though I was tempted to prolong my being waited on. After work, showers, and dinner I told her about how and why I ran away. I tried not to notice her expressions; I was too scared. She had a reason, I didn't. When I did look into her face, I saw, well, confusion rather than any type of conviction. She simply said "okay" then made for bed. *She must hate me now,* I thought.

Echo lay down beneath the blanket and then yawned and scratched her arm. "Come on, silly boy," she nearly whispered.

I did as I was told, cuddling up close to her, for fear that maybe tomorrow she wouldn't want me near her. She sighed, and we went to sleep.

I dreamed of my dad smiling at me from the window of a town car, blue maybe. Slipping slightly, Echo saw me as my eyes open a bit.

"I figured it out," she whispered in the dark, waking me from a half sleep. "At first I was angry, because I would give anything to have parents that love me, but then I got to wondering." She sighed and put her hand on mine. "It's destiny, if you had no reason and did it anyway. It has to be." She smiled, closing the gap between our lips. After a pause she concluded, "Think about it. I'll try to be as strong as I can for you, no matter what you decide."

I knew then that her love went beyond herself. She loved all of me, for me, outside her own desires. I felt as though I had woken to find myself in a fairytale romance. What made her love me anyway? I can't imagine deserving it.

Oddly, I didn't hurt inside anymore. My deliberation was thoughtful, not painful. Echo had lifted the shadow and injected the anesthetic, and I was forever in her debt.

I watched her in the dark, straining my pupils to catch every bit of light as she drifted away from me. The world outside was quiet, then another car passed, a silent song waiting, in the dark between us. I tried to listen as my memory saw, but all I could hear was a hum outside.

There was a click of the clasp on the gate. *Why is Dad here so late?* I carefully detangled myself and slipped on my coat, which was hanging next to the door. Dad never came so late. In the still, warm dark of the apartment, I was afraid. Quietly I opened the door, slipped out, and closed it behind me. As I navigated the stairs, I heard the engine cut. The truck door creaked a little when it opened, and I made haste to round the building as not to startle him in the dark without the truck's dome light. Looking as though he half expected me, he shoved the door shut and whispered as well as any grown man could.

"Sorry if I woke you up."

"Nah, couldn't sleep," I replied gently

"Me neither."

Wordlessly we entered the seclusion of Dad's studio, and he made for the light switch. He paused as the fluorescent bulb flickered to life then retrieved from a box near the rear of the building a beer.

"Want one?" Dad asked in an almost foreboding tone.

"Sure," I responded in an unintended echo. I met him halfway to receive the law-breaking contribution. Then we retired to the couch.

"What's your dad like?" Roy inquired with some intended direction. He twisted the bottle's cap and leaned back into the cushions.

"Well," I thought, following his lead, "like a lot of dads, I imagine." I sipped tastelessly on the cheap, warm beer.

"My father was a real asshole." He ignored the mild expression of surprise as it seized my face momentarily. He took a deep swallow before continuing. "Through my relentless, continual efforts, I have managed to not become him. I try to be the father I needed. I'm always trying to be better." He paused and looked at me with tearing green eyes, but I couldn't think of what to say. My sympathy could draw no warm conclusion. "My son acts as though I'm a terrible father. He doesn't listen to me. If I were my father, I'd knock the crap out of him instead of trying to reason and understand." He took a few more swallows of beer. "I try so hard." He said, wiping tears from his eyes.

If anyone in the world ever felt like a total asshole, it was me. As if I was a stranger to my own father, remorse, and my own shame.

"If he could see through your eyes, he wouldn't be able to treat you that way. Everyone has faults, even your son." I laid my hand on his shoulder. "Don't take his youthful convictions as faults of your own. He's got a lot to learn about the world, most of which he's gonna have to learn for himself. He'll appreciate you someday. Just keep doing what you know is right."

Roy looked at me and gave a half grin. "What makes you so sure?"

"Cuz my dad's a good guy, and I've put him through hell." Roy refocused his attention on me. "I'm suddenly aware of what I've done."

I spilled everything over the course of the early morning, each of us shedding light on one another's situation. Roy had to admit Echo and I were destined to be together, but he persuaded me to go home. He promised he'd take care of Echo, not that either of us thought she needed it. *Oh, Echo, how could I?*

113

Chapter 12

I sat next to her while watching her sleep. *How do I tell her? I am torn, trapped between my fathers' son and a child's lover. What then? If you belong to both?* She was awake, keeping her eyes closed. Was she afraid to see me? I needed her to see me now. The veils that had kept me out for so long were lifted. She smiled with this puzzling first moment.

"What are you doing? You look like crap. Did you sleep at all?" She couldn't hide that expression of knowing. She could read me like a book, and took these words from my tongue's pages. "You're going home, aren't you?"

She could never try to break my heart, but it was shattered nonetheless. "I've got to. You know I don't want to, but what's right is what's right," I nearly sobbed.

She curled her lips to smile, only to nearly cry. "I know. Don't worry about me. I'll be fine."

Echo insisted I take a bus so she wouldn't have to worry about me. I would agree to any terms she set forth. I'd stay in Olympia long enough to save up for the ticket home, then murder a piece of my soul saying good-bye. I made promises I knew I could keep: I'll keep in touch and we'll be together again soon.

I tried to slow those minutes to a crawl and stop time from passing the best I could. I memorized everything about him: every movement, sound, and mannerism that made him. How could I say it? When the time came, could I say good-bye? The days passed with me dragging my feet all the while. We were paid, the ticket was bought, and the date was printed in black ink. He would be home Christmas Eve. We had one more day in which to say it. His bus would leave in the morning.

I used the forty dollars I had been saving to take him to the arcade, where we met up with the usual suspects. Altogether, we won enough tickets to get Bon a comb that flips closed like a butterfly knife.

I tried my best to ignore Gillian's sympathy and pretend I didn't so much care Bon was leaving, but she knew us too well. It almost seemed as though it was breaking her heart to see the two of us part, not just our own.

As we moved to exit the arcade, Gillian pulled me into the bathroom. "Are you sure you're all right?" she asked.

"I guess. What am I gonna do, just die?" I reasoned honestly. She thought about it for a moment. "Be strong for me," I said. "Your sympathy is making me want to cry, and I'll have plenty of time for that when he's gone." I sighed and leaned against the metal sink. "If I cry, he'll stay, and I can't be that selfish. I'm sure his dad has done more than his fair share of crying for that boy. I guess maybe it's my turn."

Gillian's eyes welled with tears that she swept away before they could fall. "Well, if you ever need a friend, you know where to find me anytime," she noted with remorse, laying her hand on my shoulder.

"Thanks." I smiled, moving toward the exit.

"Do you think you'll do it tonight?" she asked with a giggle. It took me a moment to realize what she was referring to.

I blushed; I had been so busy trying to slow time that I hadn't thought that far ahead. "I suppose we should," I remarked with a blank and thoughtful stare at the door.

"Yeah!" Gillian laughed.

We left the restroom in nervous giggles.

Taking up contributions, we managed pizza and beer. We brought it all back to the apartment for a farewell party, only to wear away at those precious hours. My face wore pleasant shades of make-upped emotion, but my heart was suffocating. Even though he was here with me, I missed him in anticipation of missing him. Everyone was laughing, having a great time, ticking into the evening. It wasn't until after three in the morning that we managed to chase everyone out. When they were gone, I didn't know what to do.

A ten minute shower with my toothbrush, and I lay in bed, in the dark, next to an equally awkward Bon. Like old strangers in all-too-familiar situations, we started with what we had perfected, kisses—long, hungry kisses. We forgot about the rest of the world, about people, problems, and time. As I had suspected, my heart stopped when Bon unbuttoned my pajama top. So dizzy, so in love, we held tight to one another.

So absorbed in these moments it seemed as though I had mastered time; it had stopped, lost in a kiss. Decision out of desire, I began to work my underwear to my knees. As Bon moved in closer, there came a knock at the door. Virginity intact, we scrambled in giggles to make ourselves presentable.

It was Dad who came to take Bon to the bus station. I opened the door while Bon calmed down and we apologized for "sleeping in." I helped Bon gather his things, insisting he take the guitar but leave me Azazel. He left me his bag with the camp gear, compass, and atlas. I rode along and helped him anticipate his bus.

We waited for the first one to speak, the bus at idle and our thoughts racing. I couldn't say it.

"I'll see you real soon, love." I put my arms around his neck to hide my tearing eyes. "When you come back, we'll find somewhere to hide where no one can find us." I gave an inexperienced wink, and we both blushed a little.

I love yous, I'll miss yous, but not a single good-bye, and then he was gone. I felt so lonely.

Dad tried to cheer me up, but all I wanted to do was hide somewhere till it stopped hurting. How long could this terrible feeling last? I knew what I had to do: make time pass as quickly as possible. Like T.S. Elliot wrote, distracted from distraction by distraction, I'd have to find as many distractions as I could. I'd start tomorrow; today I would wallow in the wreathing loneliness.

I went home, locked the door, and cried. I drew a bath and sat in it till it was cold. I couldn't eat or sleep, but I could cry till my eyes were swollen and dry. I was missing half of me. I had thought he'd always be by my side.

Hard work and beer filled the empty space he left inside of me. I forced the corners of my lips to conclude the illusion I'd be all right. I'm always all right. My hands itched and ached to hold him. I missed his breath on the back of my neck while we slept. I spent Christmas drunk under a bridge, alone and singing ill-remembered lyrics to carols I never understood. I wrote several letters, sending only the pleasant percentage, and received letter upon letter in return. Letters of love and apologies. I cried with every one, as if saying to the sky and earth, "But we love each other! We love each other!"

When void of the next obligation, I went out walking, picking the half-smoked cigarettes out of ashtrays, giving myself an addiction for distraction. Effectively taking my thoughts from me, I seemed to be safely numbing over.

Dad enrolled me in high school, passing me off as one of his own. It was hard at first, trying to catch up, but with Gillian's help I became a B student. I studied to keep myself occupied and even sent home a copy of my report card with the location information blacked out. I imagined that they probably wouldn't be proud, but maybe at least surprised. My uncle was so proud of me; in a letter he told me how he knew I was bright all along.

Time began to stumble forward, and I didn't hurt so badly anymore. I was saving money and looking forward to summer.

I had a family now, scattered but fundamentally sound. Dad was always there for me when I needed him, and even when I didn't, giving me a lecture when I came to work hungover or stayed out too late. All my friends became close as siblings, or closer. Gillian and I were nearly inseparable. She started work with me at the hotel, and we spent the night at each other's houses constantly. Ben was my drinkin' buddy. Every Friday night we found a place, got a bottle, and drank with friends or acquaintances. Courtney came and went from the group of friends, but I always loved her when she was around. The older group—Brad, Matt, Kim, Jared, Lauren, Benjamin, and Josh—were always happy to see me and always game for fun. We made cheesy horror films, conspired, and printed zines, and I sent copies of them to Bon. We found as many ways to pass the time as we could think of. I found out that I'm exceptional at a lot of things. I'm good with a can of spray paint, and I only got better with instruction from Matt. My zine articles were talked about, and I became locally famous for them. Everyone wanted me to play a major role anytime we made a movie, claiming I was a wicked actress. I felt so loved, though I couldn't help but feel somewhat sheltered. Outside of smokes, pot, and alcohol I was excluded. I picked up on drug references alluding to mushrooms, ecstasy, acid, and opium but they wouldn't expose me. I supposed I was too young or only acted naive and mildly offended.

My zine articles centered on social classes that high school students stick themselves in. I wrote about music and sometimes politics. There were a lot of girls inspired by my rants; they knew me, but I hadn't a clue as to what their names might have been. I felt a little bad but strangely flattered. I was impermeable and strong, a legend in my own right, and I knew it was because no one really knew me. I was a beautiful shell that no one could infiltrate.

School ended, and Gillian and I felt electric. We had to work, but we had plans for later. It was warm, and we had a date with a bong, a thirty-pack, and a pack of Camel Wides. We were all going to meet up at Jared's dead grandma's house to celebrate the end of the school year (which Gillian and I agreed was strange, considering the people throwing the party had dropped out of school over two years ago).

We rushed through work as fast as we could, giggling about our expectations for the evening. Would Brad get drunk and put the moves on Courtney again? What music should we bring?

We clocked out at ten and went to my apartment to give each other a make-under, washing off the eyeliner and shadow, changing into dirty jeans, tank tops, boots, and long-sleeve button ups. We were ready!

Ben picked us up in his sister's small truck, and we crammed all three of us in the front bench seat. We parked a block away so as not to arouse suspicion. When we arrived, it looked vacant save for the single car in the driveway and the murmur of music. We knocked, but there was no answer, so we double-checked the address and let ourselves in. Light spilled from the doorway onto the cement porch, yet from the exterior, it appeared to be unlit. The music was much louder as well, like nothing I had ever heard before—not like any of my bands. The front room was empty, void of furniture except for a small child's foldout chair. The front window had been soundproofed with blankets stapled to the frame and a thick layer of black paint on the panes themselves.

I followed Ben and Gillian down the hall adjacent to the kitchen. The carpet was purple shag, and the walls were a worn white. The door was cracked open a half inch to the back bedroom, where the music was pouring out. Ben slowly pushed the door and we were greeted by faces and voices I couldn't yet identify. We shuffled into the cramped room. Everyone was there, producing the notes I had never heard in a haze of pot and cigarette smoke. Courtney sat on the PA speaker near the far left corner next to Brad, and Gillian gave me a knowing laugh as Courtney called us over. Stepping between bottles, ashtrays, music sheets, a mic stand, and a keyboard, we made it over to her to receive a warm smile and a cheap can of beer.

"Echo" was hollered hoarsely from the far closet door. It was Josh, who was passing a live electric guitar my way. With some effort, I reached to receive the instrument. I opened the beer and drank in attempt to catch up. I pulled the tab from the beer can for a pick and began to play with the buzzed collection of broken instruments. Benjamin sat on a milk crate to play a collection of mismatched drums half lying on the floor. Josh improvised lyrics over a microphone. Kim rolled her fingers over the dated keyboard as she drew a long drink from a half gallon of cheap vodka and passed it to Jared, who stopped playing the purple electric to take up the bottle. The song never ended, instruments were passed, exchanged, evolving a drunken tempo change but never stopped. Groups retired to other rooms for conversation, but the song carried on. I sang for a while in a soft voice about a boy who had gone and tried my hand at playing the drums while Gillian played chopsticks on the keyboard. Benjamin mock interviewed kids with his video camera and set up strange scenes to be acted out by drunken kids. Gillian and I made a spoof commercial for the cheap beer we were drinking. Wrestling matches ensued in the living room, to the rattle of a snare drum.

As I stood back and watched them all, I felt so in love, something I didn't think was possible since Bon's departure. I was so in love with their energy as a whole. Everyone lent the best of themselves to the group. They were beautiful, and I was in awe.

We all crashed out in our respective corners in the house as the sun rose, I in the living room. As I drifted off to sleep, someone neared me, and in a whisper I identified Josh. He said, "You're radical. I'm falling for you." I pretended to remain sleeping, and he shuffled away. I was flattered but relentlessly, madly in love with Bon.

We woke in a hangover daze to Benjamin playing back the night's audio on his tape recorder. When my voice sounded on the recording, he shook his fist above his head and nodded with rock-and-roll approval.

Dad had made out four big envelopes addressed to different organizations running short story contests. He gave me an old word processor and encouraged me to type up a few of my stories and send them in. I was scared of rejection. "What have you got to lose?" he told me.

So I typed up a horror story, a tragedy of high school angst, and finally a love story. I mailed out the stories two hours before my birthday party. I would be sixteen, and all I wanted was a boy named Bon. I had received a birthday package from him two days before, a silver heart-shaped locket with a picture of him, a hundred dollars, his best wishes, and more then all that combined, his love.

Dad was hosting my party deep in the field of junk behind the studio. He bought the alcohol—tequila, rum, and champagne for my sweet sixteen. I should have been a lot more excited than I was. Although I knew better, I couldn't help but hope to see Bon. I walked home from the post office, indulging in fantasies of winning the writing contests.

When I got home, Dad was clearing out an area in the back hidden from the road by foliage and junk. He had set up two metal trash cans and filled them with wood, sticks, paper, and anything else that would burn. Dad had stopped up an old bathtub and filled it with ice, soda, and beer.

"Happy birthday!" he exclaimed, excited to see me. "Did you get them mailed off?"

His smile made me suddenly happy and anxious. "Sure did," I giggled. "Oh, I hope I win." His excitement for me made me excited for me.

"They'd have to be crazy not to pick your stories," he soothed. "Got everything just about ready for the party."

"It looks awesome. I'm sure not every girl gets to have their sweet sixteen drunk in a junk yard," I observed without sarcasm.

"You'll be the envy of all the girls," he joked.

Deep down inside, I figured no one would show up. Since Bon had left, my low self-esteem had come creeping back in.

Gillian was the first to arrive, early and over prepared as usual. "I brought streamers and hotdog stuff," she announced, making her way across the path through the junk.

"Wicked," I replied, moving to help her unpack the large blue backpack.

We hung the streamers from the tallest of obstructions, a refrigerator, a couple of trees, and a sagging phone line. As we worked, people started pouring in, many more than I had expected. Most came with party contributions and some with birthday gifts.

Dad ran an extension cord and brought out a stereo. He picked through his private collection of tapes and CDs to deejay the party with dated rock we all knew the words to.

The sun was setting, and I was catching a buzz. Beautiful. My guests were following suit and drinking with smiles on their faces.

In my inebriated trance, in the full of the moon, I heard it. A soft voice whispering in my ear on another frequency entirely. "Happy Birthday, baby." A voice I knew better than the beating of my own heart. The air softly smelled of him, from a message sent on the moon.

Chapter 13

I felt it; she could hear me. As I sat in the dark of the back yard, our longing had forged a bridge through the night sky. We were somehow together there for a moment, and I wondered if I was crazy.

I had been my father's best Christmas present. He cried, and my guilt ate a hole though the souls of my shoes. Chained to my guilt, I tried to go through the motions of settling in, but it felt like a lie. I was always lonely. The only thing that consoled me was the satisfaction derived from doing the right thing and comforting my father. When I left again to be with Echo, I wanted his blessing. Due to my docile, consenting nature, I wasn't forced to see a shrink. I honestly didn't need one this time anyway; Echo had cured me with love. I was serving my sentence. I could never be home, not if she wasn't there.

My dad planned to enroll me in public school, thinking that making friends would keep me here. I had a few friends, but Dad wasn't all too approving of them. Jack, for instance, was seventy five and liked to play chess and argue. I would often meet him at the café downtown to indulge his good nature with a few games. I loved that man. I liked to hang out with Sidney, who was in his late twenties and had dropped too much acid in high school, leaving him poetically crazy. He was a liar by nature but a gentle soul. He would get me going every once in a while till I remembered that facts to him were subject to an abstract interpretation. May, the librarian, had a wealth of knowledge and was a beautiful conversationalist. I had friends.

Indebted as I felt toward my father, I agreed to public school, though I feared it might bring me too close to mediocrity.

I had gotten a job working in a coffee shop making lattes and sandwiches for strangers who were rushing to their graves. Why is it that the closer people get to death, the faster they try to get there? There was a plan in motion. I was in the process of getting my driver's license and saving money for a car. I planned to ride in and sweep Echo off her feet. It should be white, my car, just like that legendary steed. Then we're off into the sunset.

Whenever I lay down under the roof of my father's house to sleep, I replayed the days spent with Echo. I tried to remember everything that happened, anything that gave us a smile to share. Every single memory became incredibly important, and I played them over and over in my mind to ensure they never faded.

Lovers and madmen keep much in common, and I was madly in love. I imagined her smiling in the summer sun, the wind blowing through her hair, and her smiling at me.

The summer stayed its course, lost in overtime, love letters, and cheap beer. I anticipated through the month the judging of my short stories and paid handsomely for a ride into the city at least once a week to check the PO box. I started to give up hope. Roy, in attempting to console me, admitted that I would be amongst the youngest to have entered the contest. How could I compete with people with life experience twice my own? I let it go without a whimper, knowing what I would grow to write someday.

Having accepted my defeat gracefully, I was stunned to recover a foreign envelope from my PO box on Wednesday afternoon. Roy had driven me to the post office, teasing me for my love letter expectations. He found it strange Bon and I still wrote so feverishly. Roy sat in the truck, and my emotions collided as I pondered my next actions. As soft as I knew my heart was, I feared and anticipated the contents of the letter. If it was a polite rejection, I world cry and be embarrassed in front of Dad, but if it was an award, I would want to share it with him. I clutched two letters against my chest as I made my contemplations. *Coffee,* I decided. I would read Bon's letter first to calm me, and then I would read the sorted one. When I returned to Dads' truck, he immediately noticed the tension distracting me. He greeted me with a coy, wise smile.

"Coffee," I said once inside the cab.

"Anything you want, miss *New York Times* best seller," he replied as he started the engine.

With those words, my anxiety turned to excitement, and I realized what Roy already knew: there was no sense in dread without cause. I should expect the best. If I opened the envelope and it was bad, at least I would enjoy opening it, right?

Dad stopped at the next coffee shop, and this being Seattle, it took only moments. Its walls were shared with hundreds of books that seemed to yawn at us as we entered the aromatic establishment. The pretty barista smiled at us from behind an old-fashioned cash register.

"Take a seat. I'll get the coffee," Dad insisted. I did so without objection. When I sat down on the worn seat of a wooden chair, I realized I was still clutching the letters tightly to my heart. I released my grip and gently laid them out in front of me on the small, round, wooden table. I needed Bon with me now; I needed that calm, collected nature he always seemed to radiate. I picked up the letter from him and carefully opened it. The usual beauty poured from the handwritten pages. Of course, there were butterflies in my stomach as those poetic words seemed almost whispered in my ear.

Dad returned with two little cups of espresso. "I'm not sure what I just ordered," he admitted quietly to me. I discreetly allowed the generation gap to amuse me, giving a little giggle. "So, how's Bon doing?" he asked, and I fluttered to report that he missed me while serving his time with the best of spirits.

"P.S. Good luck with the writing contest, though with the way you write, you needn't any luck, just a competent reader," were Bon's last words. I was inflamed with flattery. I gently refolded Bon's letter and tucked it back into the envelope.

Now the moment had come. I took a sip of the hot espresso, smiled at Dad, and began to open the letter. Dad could hardly stay in his seat, and I wondered if he had polished off the thick soup of coffee.

The letter was printed on a fine, light-tan paper. My heart jumped, figuring it probably contained more cotton than my shirt. It was folded precisely into thirds. I lifted the first fold up. Roy leaned in closer. The next fold down, a slip of paper fluttered to the floor. As Roy bent to pick it up with a thrilled laugh, my eyes scanned the letter. *Congratulations, second place, love story.* I let out a sigh and let the news engulf me. The feeling was huge. All I could do was giggle.

"Five hundred dollars," Dad informed me with a nudge and a smile. I couldn't believe it. How the hell did I manage so much? I couldn't have without Bon, my muse. I handed Dad the letter and inspected the check. *Wow, five hundred,* I kept telling myself.

Dad began to laugh, almost in hysterics. He tried to calm himself. "Did you read this?" he laughed. "They say you might well have a future as a writer but not as an orthographer, because your spelling is terrible."

In disbelief I leaned to eye the letter. Dad pointed out the passage, and we both laughed. Mrs. Barker, my old English teacher always told me that writers had to be good spellers. In her face!

Using my school ID, I cashed the check. Dad and I had pizza on me before driving back home. I slept on daydreamed clouds that night, pretending Bon was with me.

I checked the mail every day, receiving each letter as though it were the first in years. She wrote every week, if not more often. I hungered for her handwriting in a silly way, my favorite pain of longing.

I was enjoying the summer, spending my time reading after work in the park downtown. I found time to catch up with old friends and make a few new acquaintances; unfortunately, none of them was noteworthy.

One sunny late afternoon I sat reading a new novel under a tree, lost in someone else's world, when an unwanted distraction came. A shrill outburst of obnoxious laughter broke my concentration but could not bring my eyes from the page. A second voice in giggles was followed again by loud laughter. I finished the paragraph and forced my eyes up. Two girls sat at a picnic table in front of me, about fifty feet away, staring at me like a couple of gawking monkeys in a zoo. They whispered and giggled to one another then gestured in my direction. Ignoring them, I continued reading. This must have frustrated them, because they only got louder and more insistent for attention. I couldn't disappear into my reading, and they wouldn't shut up. I pondered my options. I could leave, but go where? My dad was picking me up in an hour. A disgusting idea entered into my thoughts. *Beautiful,* I thought. I pretended to continue reading but dropped the book closer to my lap. That way the girls could have a clear look at my handsome face. Acting casually as the girls continued to giggle, I lifted my hand to my face, extended my index finger, and began to pick my nose. They giggled out of disgust, and I fought the smile of satisfaction that tried creeping onto my face. I finished, wiped my finger on my pants, and lifted the book back to my face. They made murmurs but no more outbursts of retarded, attention-starved laughter.

I thought myself lucky to have so many people seeking to trip a pretty face, trying to encourage a fall. Echo and I only stumbled on destiny. We were rendered helpless but fell in love with one another. A fortunate accident we were neither seeking nor expecting. It just happened.

On occasion, to break the boredom of suburban normality, I'd treat myself to an underage consumption. My crazy friend Sidney would buy my alcohol under the penalty of a lecture, but it only lasted till he forgot what he was talking about. With a six pack of cheap beer, I'd stay up till the early morning, drawing, listening to music over my headphones, and writing letters to Echo I'd never send. The hand writing was terrible, and the subject matter sometimes became a little too passionate.

On the last Saturday of summer, to mark the occasion, I was drinking in my room again. I was all registered for school and filled with dread. I drank to insist that I forget and enjoy the last of my freedom. I finished my first beer and reflected on my antisocial behavior. I wasn't so antisocial when Echo was with me; what happened? Maybe I just met cooler people when we were together. Maybe she just made me stronger or complete. Whatever the case, I still didn't want to go to public school.

I gently cracked another beer and listened for any stirring in the house. All were in bed by ten, the whole damn neighborhood. Those feelings came back. Oh, those reasons to cause me to want to run. I pushed them away and drew faith hungrily from the beer. What was she doing right now? When could I go back to her? I would go now if only it weren't for my guilt. Oh, my guilt, laden on me like cement shoes. If only I had my father's permission, only then could I truly be free. Maybe when I turn eighteen, he'll understand and be able to let me go. Another long drink and I recalled the way she smiled when she started to feel the alcohol in her cheeks. How came her eyes to be so bright?

My face felt warm, and I killed the beer to encourage the effect. I mulled over my new school supplies—glossy new notebooks, a few binders, new mechanical pencils—and I felt despair. In awe of the things we do out of guilty love. In detest of my fellow students

128

and father, I thought of drawing swastikas all over my notebooks and school effects. A truck of cowboys intent on beating me up passed over my mind, and I thought better of my distain. I wanted to be left to my own devices when without her. An idea to soothe me: I'd bring her with me. With another beer and a set of colored magic markers, I began to breathe her to life across a notebook. I drew her in orange wearing nothing but her underwear, cradling Azazel across her stomach. Black musical notes surrounded the two of them. Along the top of the notebook, I inscribed in bold black, "Bon and Echo forever." I drank the rest of the six pack and decorated the rest of my supplies, hoping it would still be a good idea when I woke up in the morning.

When all had been done and tomorrow had come, I wished I had made my artwork a bit more masculine. I had put red hearts on my binders. My school supplies looked as though a girl had decorated them. Now all I needed was glitter. If my intentions were to make myself appear like a closeted homosexual, I had succeeded.

I used all of Sunday trying to fix my notebooks and other effects. Echo would have laughed so hard if she could see me. I snapped a few photos to send to her and relished the thought of her laughing.

In school, I was the kid who was everyone's friend but at the same time had no friends. In class I was pleasant and talkative, but I hid away to eat my lunch alone. This suited me.

For the first time in my life, I was excited to be going back to school. Now that I wasn't drowning in homework I couldn't understand, I was eager to learn new things. Gillian didn't share my enthusiasm; I was alone on this one. I'm the girl that everyone knew but that didn't know anybody, save for the friends Bon and I had forged together. I was constantly being harassed by the staff for wearing my headphones in the hallways, spreading zines, and doodling my love for Bon on my notebooks. It touched me to know Bon, too, had plastered his thoughts of me on his school stuff. If I couldn't help be silly over him, it helped to know he was silly for me.

Life was flying by, and I wanted it to. I went to school, and then to work. I managed to write the zine, make another movie, and drink with friends. The more I could cram in, the better, because the faster time went by, the sooner I would be able to see his smile again. Every night, when I hit my pillow exhausted, I fell asleep immediately in anticipation. When I abandoned myself for dreams, he was there, perfect, the way only a lover's eye could perceive. The way he walked, the freckles on his cheeks, but most of all the life in those eyes, electric and unyielding. If there is a god, I knew she loved him, because we had been led to be together. There was nothing I wouldn't do for him. God must love me too, to lead him to me. In dreams we made love the way we always had, hopped trains, shared a novel, and held hands. In my long waking hours, I sometimes looked at my palms, wondering why they literally ached to touch him. I thought maybe I had carpel tunnel syndrome, but the feeling faded away when I could recall my dreams upon waking. The pain was gone until my hands forgot what his hands felt like, and I dreaded that they shouldn't hurt upon forgetting his touch. I had been told that love is nothing more than compatible pheromones, but I can't bring myself to believe that. This love, and love like it, had given birth to religion, brought down crooked nations, and parented innocents.

Chapter 14

When I woke, confusion set in momentarily. When my eyes were closed, he was there, but when I woke, oh, it was like watching him get on that bus again. I pushed aside the heartache and got ready for the day.

It was Thursday, and I was ready for my English test. I didn't have to study; I was so enlightened with the section of poetry we had covered (I had already immersed myself in some of it) that I knew it front to back.

Gillian picked me up in her mom's car, and we followed in our footprints of a habitual day. Geometry followed by science, but at lunch I felt sick. Relentlessly it pursued me. I strangely felt like running, complete with a knot in my stomach that reminded me of the last night at my uncle's house.

Gillian must have noticed my discomfort because she kept staring at me, looking puzzled.

"What's wrong?" she eventually asked, resting her head against her locker with a thud.

Lately we spent lunch breaks sitting in the hallway resisting the urge to bum smokes in the parking lot.

"I don't know, but I can't seem to shake it. I feel like shit," I replied, peeling the label from my soda bottle. I stared down the hallway monitor as he walked by before continuing. "I've got that feeling something's wrong. Maybe I'm just getting sick."

"Do you think you need to go home?" she sympathized.

"Yeah," I responded, to Gillian's surprise.

As the bell rang to return to class, I wrote myself a sick note, gave it to Gillian to turn in, and made my way home. Roy's handwriting was blissfully easy to forge, so I feared no repercussions.

Halfway home I was consumed with the urge to run, and having learned to follow my instincts, I did. Like a kite, I followed home the mile and a half of line. Nothing amiss, nor was it unordinary. The feeling wouldn't ebb. The overcast driveway was empty, the gate was locked. Why must I run?

Awkwardly I fumbled my way to the apartment, packed all Bon's bag could hold, the Roy original, photos, my ship in a bottle, Azazel, the road atlas, and my story book. I threw in my favorite extra set of clothes and topped off the bag with food that wouldn't spoil and the tiny camp stove. Half in a daze, I worked without a clue as to why. I kept telling myself I was crazy. Had I had too much caffeine? I sat on the bed to try and calm myself and breathe deeply. It helped. *What the fuck is wrong with me?* My thoughts senselessly made circles like a dog chasing its tail, pointing to one end: destination nowhere. Beside myself in phantom fear, I went outside for fresh air. I walked down the stairs, content to take my time.

Intending on bedding my fears to rest, I peeked around the corner to the front gate. To my surprise, there was a black car parked outside the fence. As I studied the car, I noted the spotlight by the side mirror, the cage that separated the back from the front seat, and the officer talking over the CB. My heart sank.

"Shit," I whispered turning to head back up stairs. "How the hell did they find me?" Strangely, once the cause of my unease was identified, I relaxed. I meandered up the stairs to retrieve my belongings and glanced around to ensure I left no personal, undeniable evidence. I feared Roy might feel heat from harboring a runaway and I felt remorse. He didn't deserve that.

Olympia is no longer my home, I thought as I closed the apartment door behind me for the last time. I set out across the field of junk, keeping the officer's line of sight obstructed. I was too bummed out to be scared. *Who turned me in? Could the police be here for any other reason? What the hell am I supposed to do now?* One thing I knew: I had to say good-bye to Gillian.

I kept a low profile, snuck into the student parking lot at the school, and got into Gillian's mom's car. I lay down on the floor of the back seat and covered myself with Bon's backpack and one of Gillian's jackets. There I waited as patiently as I could, bored and livid and brooding. There were no likely suspects, and that's what was bothering me. I had no one to blame, no direction in which to cast my anger.

I was convinced that by now, my parents had given up and forgotten about me. Maybe they remembered me once a year while filing taxes with a stab of regret when shy a dependent. I was at a frustrated standstill. *Who the hell told?*

On the verge of exploding, my anger was momentarily dulled by the muffled sound of the school bell. I anxiously waited for Gillian, hearing the gradual filtration of students into the parking lot, giggles, hollers and the roaring of old engines. I could hear the scuffling of her feet, a dainty dragging that only she could do. She sighed after opening the door. She plopped down into the seat, slammed the door, and rested her head back. There was a jingle of keys in the ignition.

"Gillian," I said quietly, trying not to startle her, but I did anyway.

"Echo?" she nearly yelled. "Oh, my god, there were some cops looking for you. Are you okay?"

"I'm fine but confused."

"How the hell did you know? Right after you left, they showed up and started pulling kids out of class, asking questions. I played dumb, but I think that asshole Kenny opened his mouth."

"Kenny," I mouthed. That freak, the psychotic stalker who played to have a crush on me. He had followed me home on two separate occasions that I was aware of and tried to infiltrate the flanks of my friend family, but he was rejected. I could see that snake talking when confronted with a cop, but to ninety-nine percent of the school, I was Roy's daughter, not a runaway. If he had called the cops in the first place, they would have been waiting for me at home, not drilling kids for information at the school. Still, he was the one I could deal out my retribution to, poor slob.

"I had that bad feeling, went home, packed my stuff, and found a hide-a-cop in my driveway." I shuffled out from under the bag and jacket but stayed on the floor. "Let's get out of the parking lot."

"Oh, shit, duh," Gillian said beginning to back up.

We swung by Courtney's house. Gillian ran in and returned moments later. Courtney was slinging questions from the open doorway, and Gillian promised to explain later. We could have taken Courtney with us, but with as much love as we had for her, we could never trust her. She was a beautiful flake. Gillian opened the car door a bit, threw me a wad of something soft, and hopped in. I found my way into an oversized black dress as Gillian pulled out of the driveway and headed down the street.

Wearing a shoulder-length blonde wig, I jumped into the front seat, where Gillian handed me a pair of retro, black-rimmed sunglasses. Figuring my disguise only made me stand out, I sat low in the passenger seat.

"Where should we go?" Gillian asked with an unmasked tone of rebellious excitement.

"Do you know where Kenny lives?" was my dark reply.

She gave a nervous giggle. "I'm not sure which house, but I know what street."

"Let's go there."

We drove in a short spell of silence till Gillian lamented. "I'll keep you like this, forever incognito. We could give you an accent and say you're my cousin from Ireland." She tried to believe it could work. I gave a dismissive smile, knowing she knew.

"Maybe I could go with you," she noted, offering up her courage. I must admit, I wanted her with me. I was scared to go alone, and she always felt like home, but it couldn't be.

"Your dad would hunt me down and keep my head as a trophy," I responded, denying myself the bliss of such an accomplice. I couldn't resist wishing she had come from worse circumstances to justify my taking her away. "When you're eighteen, you can run away to come see me. I'll let you know where I am by then."

She seemed remorsefully relieved at the alternative suggestion, and my heart sank a little.

"There he is!" I exclaimed, locking my eyes on that son of a bitch. Kenny was still walking home from school, blue backpack in tow. Gillian circled the block and came up slowly behind him. He glanced over at us and guiltily slowed his pace. I took off the wig and sunglasses then called to him. He smiled a devil's smile and continued to walk. I got out of the car and followed him, calling to him once more, but he broke into a run. I gave chase. He turned right and then left up an alley. I gained quickly, in a dress no less, and seized the handle of his backpack, pulling him down.

"Why are you running from me?" I panted. "Did you fucking tell them? Did you, you piece of shit?"

Stunned, he got to his feet. "The truth will set you free," he smirked.

I lost my decorum and laid him out with a fisted shot to his nose. He writhed on the gravel, clutching his face.

"Get up, asshole!" I shouted.

He pulled his hand away from his nose, cupping a pool of blood. Streaming over his lips and dripping endlessly from his chin, his blood spattered the rocky ally floor.

"You broke my nose, you fucking bitch!" he roared, dizzily trying to sit up properly.

"You deserve more. Now get up!"

He weakly threw a handful of gravel at me that failed to get a response.

"Echo!" Gillian called from the end of the alley.

135

"You took everything from me," I told him calmly. "My home, my family, my future." Although it disagreed with my principals, I kicked him hard in his side as he sat helpless. He fell to the gravel again, struggling to breathe. I sprinted down the alley to where Gillian waited, car ready.

"The cops are undoubtedly on their way," she said as I got into the car. We pulled out, and I resumed my new identity as a blonde.

"That prick got what he deserved," she said, sounding as if she were trying to convince herself.

"Can you bring me to the edge of town, near the train tracks?" I asked with more somber notes than intended. She responded wordlessly with her soft brown eyes. We traveled as though in a funeral procession morning the inevitable loss of one another.

Few words were spoken before she left me alone beside the intersection of road and tracks. I had promised to write when it was safe and told her to tell everyone good-bye for me, plus apologize to Roy and send him my love and gratitude. I watched her disappear in her mother's car through the tinted lenses of my disguise.

Another home lost. I felt more alone now than ever before. I began to walk up the tracks, ever farther from those who loved me. The sky opened and cold drops began to fall, mingling with my tears.

"I wanna go home," I cried to the wind, but I knew damn well I'd never really had one. I felt pitied, as though god were crying for me with every drop that fell to dampen my hair and cheeks and shoulders. Without a soul to hear me, I let my defenses falter and then fail. I cried loudly and cursed fate for the wounds that jaded me. The rain fell harder, and the wind blew faster, as if carrying me away on a god's whispered apology.

I walked and walked, the rain fell, the wind blew, and night descended. To spite my aching feet, in the rain and darkness I continued to walk for hours consumed in painful thoughts. By dawn, mentally fatigued and on the verge of collapsing, an angel came. Trumpeting his arrival via train whistle, I hid in the brush to avoid the conductor's gaze. I picked a suitable coal car and hopped the train. The familiarity quieted my fears and lulled me to sleep.

When the alarm clock buzzed on the cluttered nightstand, the feeling was still there. Empty and sick. I had hardly slept in the night, and now I had to go to school. At breakfast, my father was strangely absent and distant, as if wanting to break bad news, but he remained quiet.

Echo was relentlessly in my thoughts. I could feel her; wherever she was, she was cold, and my hands were chilled trying to warm her. With nothing but fantasies to base my illness on, I had to follow a normal day.

As my father drove me to school, he kept eyeing me as I rubbed my hands on my jeans, attempting to warm them.

"Echo is cold," I finally told him, assuming he would think me crazy. He said nothing, stiffening his posture and fixing his eyes on the road ahead. I thought nothing much of it.

I felt a little better as the day wore on, or simply got use to feeling ill. My acquaintances kept asking if I was okay, and I got better at "feeling okay." Stealing myself from my thoughts' company, I lost myself in the task at hand. I sped through the hours of coffee shop labor, took the bus home, and did my homework. My father remained unyielding, so I wasted my Friday night making myself approachable. He remained quiet and in his thoughts. I spent my weekend in bed, at work, or awaiting the postman in vain. My stomach hurt, and there never came any Pepto-Bismol in the mail. I wrote her a few letters but knew it would take days before they reached Seattle. Then how long before she checked the PO box? I needed to hear from her. By Sunday night I could take it no more.

Using my father's computer I looked up Roy's phone number and called him.

"Hello?"

"Hey, Roy," I responded.

"Bon?" he exclaimed. "Is Echo all right?"

I felt the bile lurch within my empty stomach. My heart stopped, and my throat burned. My worst fears realized in just a few syllables.

I took a few moments of silence to find myself. "I haven't heard from her. What happened?"

"Cops showed up at the school looking for her. Some kid tipped them off, and they called me to come let them onto the property." He sighed heavily. "She must have known something was up, cuz by the time I got there to show the pigs around, she was packed up and long gone." Roy laughed nervously. "She broke the kid's nose that ratted on her then skipped town. I figured she would have got in touch with you."

"No. I had a bad feeling though. Have you any idea how they found out she was in Olympia?"

"The cops said they got an anonymous tip, and not from her parents. They were shocked to hear that she had been located." Roy breathed deeply. "Who knows?"

I gave Roy my father's phone number in the event she turned up or he found out anything. He promised to phone, and we said our good-byes.

I felt so helpless. What could I do? My suspicions aroused anger inside of me, and I pondered my next move. I went to my room and pulled open my bottom drawer to find my letters disheveled. My heart raced with vexation and betrayal. *My own father! Why?* I needed to ponder this pain awhile, figure it out before I said anything.

I restlessly lay on my mattress staring endlessly at the ceiling long after the lights had all but faded. The house was quiet, but my heart was far from settled, it trembled, ached and fell apart inside my chest. Where was she? My tears grew cold on my cheeks, and yet they streamed to soak my pillow. Not a sound passed my lips; my breath was tied in knots that burned my throat. My little girl was somewhere alone in this crazy world. I had taught her well, but still it tore me up and shook me to imagine my angel alone, all alone. My soul could dissipate at the thought.

I knew my dad had played the key in Echo's discovery. It was my fault that he felt he needed to. I made no secret of my love for her nor of my plans to find her after graduation. How far is fair? My father only wanted to keep me here, but this betrayal could ruin both Echo and me. I hadn't a clue as to my next move. Should I confront my father? It seemed as though his own conscience was getting to him. I would lay in wait, I decided, and let his guilt reveal the truth. As my heart ached to hear it from the conspirator's mouth, my innocence too naive to grasp such deceit, I would wait.

Oh, god, how it hurt. My mind was on fire to find her. I could just leave, I knew, but what were the chances of my finding her? I didn't even know which direction she headed. Would she feed herself to lions and come here? Part of me wished she would but knew she wasn't that daft. My deliberation caused me pain, and I writhed to find an answer. I would have to wait. Jesus, stalemated again. If patience is a virtue, there is none more virtuous than I.

Chapter 15

I had covered an impressive expanse of terrain since leaving Olympia. I planned my route using Bon's atlas, taking mostly trains till I was a safe distance from Washington. Once I hit the highways, I discovered quickly a profound pity for blondes. I stashed the wig in my bag; it seemed to be a beacon for creeps. Lonely men looking for young company seemed drawn to my blonde wig like flies to shit. I had declined several rides in self-preservation. Ditching the wig had helped, but I wasn't out of the woods yet. I was approached by a man in a convenience store while I ate nachos. He tried to lure me with promises of a hotel room and beer. I rudely declined his inappropriate offer by telling him that if he didn't depart immediately, I would call the police, testify, and make it my personal crusade to insure he would be Bubba's ragdoll in the state penitentiary. Needless to say, he left me alone.

My outburst impressed me. I knew it was because I was finally sick of feeling like a victim and was prepared to do something about it. Too mortified and angry to finish my lunch, I purchased a roll of duct tape, scissors, and a travel razor from the small store. I grabbed my bag and locked myself in the bathroom. I taped my boobs flat to my chest, cut my hair as close to my scalp as possible, and then used the razor to even it out. I changed into my loose t-shirt and practiced my boy voice in the mirror. Traveling got easier, though I spent more time trying to find rides.

As I made my way east, it gradually got colder. The days grew steadily longer but couldn't yet break winter's grip, which clung to the agricultural communities I passed through. Snow stubbornly fell, and my trek to cross the state became more difficult. I was going to Chicago, where I could stay with Kelly for a while. Bon would inevitably know to look for me there, I hoped, eventually.

My anger was lost to the cold and my urgency to make it to Kelly's. I wondered if she would recognize me. I hardly knew myself. I wished I would have left some hair—god, I was cold. My long jeans dragged across the highway's paved shoulder, soaking my legs like a wick. I daydreamed of our hut on the beach, sand castles, and seashells. Ah, I felt warmer.

I found myself wandering an empty highway at dusk, so cold and alone. The heavy red clouds threatened to bring more snow, and I came to the terrifying realization that I would have to stay the night out here. I was going to die tonight. There wasn't a town in sight and I only had flat fields for company. I was already numb from my toes to my bald head. The temperature steadily dropped, and all I could do was walk. Before the last trace of discernible light disappeared, I found sanctuary. A metal pipe protruded from the right bank of the highway. I made haste, nearly tumbling on frozen feet down the hill. The pipe was four feet in diameter and ran the width of the highway.

The pipe was blissfully dry in most places, and I cautiously explored it's length by lighter light. On my return from its far mouth, I collected anything that would burn that had been washed into the pipe in past years' rains. Sticks, dry weeds, newspapers, a t-shirt, and by good fortune, a wood and leather clog-style shoe.

I mothered a small fire near the entrance and began to thaw. As the feeling in my skin returned, I felt giddy. I laughed for no reason and made light of my situation. I stayed up late, finding companionship in the smoky fire. I told it stories and talked to it while it gave me life. I figured my brain must have been frostbitten.

Sweet dreams filled my mind as I slept that night, and I felt safe, finding rejuvenation upon waking.

With my last four stamps, I sent four letters: one to my love, sending my soul and confusion; to Roy, my apologies; to my uncle Steve, all that was left of my composure; and the last to Gillian, all my fears. In the letters I promised to divulge my location upon my eighteenth birthday. It was only a year and a half away; I could wait to live till then.

My eyes ached to behold something other than frozen farm fields. Cities and towns seemed to be the only things that emerged from the flat horizon. I imagined that if I were a bird, I would live here, with so much sky. I looked forward to the sun's first and last breaths, which always pulled a sigh from me.

The small portion of Iowa I experienced after leaving South Dakota left me no new impression. My weary eyes longed for something familiar, and they seemed to reject everything else. When I had finally reached Illinois, frozen, I rejoiced. A song slipped through my lips despite my efforts, and as the flavor sweetened, the song grew louder. I knew Kelly would welcome me with open arms.

I hopped a train I hoped would take me all the way to Chicago. My stomach fluttered, and I felt excitedly intimidated as I studied the street map of the city. It was huge. Having come from a small town in Colorado, I was unable to relate. Bon had always done the navigating, and I merely followed. Now that I was on my own, I felt trepidation. It was a welcome change from loneliness that had been endlessly resonating in my mind.

Travel was cold and slow. I was wearing every article of clothing I owned, yet I was still so cold. It was now March, and I had spent three weeks traveling since leaving Olympia. Anxious for spring's mild weather, I shivered through the nights and slept with what warmth the failing sun could provide.

Why am I so damned cold all the time? This is Arizona! For weeks I had been taking my temperature, assuming I must've been sick. I felt fine outside of being cold and worried. My father thought I was crazy, making it all up as a ploy to be difficult. I figured he was merely excusing his guilt with denial.

Two days ago, I woke up to my father shouting over the phone. "He doesn't know where the little bitch went," and "I won't allow you to drag my son into the middle of this." Had I not been so cold, I would have pulled the blankets off and confronted him.

It had to be Echo he was talking about. Where was she? Why was I so cold?

I woke to the cold of the setting sun and made my breakfast of hot instant oatmeal over the Sterno stove. I watched the sun disappear, taking with it the last traces of light, and considered my options. I could read over old letters, listen to Azazel cry for as long as a station would come in, or reread my Rod McKuen poetry book. I huffed. That's what I had been doing for the past few days, and I was bored with my prospects.

I sat awhile in deliberation then decided to climb and sit on the top of the train car. It was always colder up there, so I normally refrained, but this time I figured it would help me wake up. Slowly and ever so carefully, I mounted the icy ladder, leaving my bag strapped to the platform. From the outside of the ladder, I mounted each rung cautiously and made my way to the top. Once my head rose above the train car's roof, my heart jumped and rejoiced. I scrambled the rest of the way up and sat facing into the wind. There on the horizon was a miniature metropolis, small enough to squish between my fingers, all twinkling lights like precious jewels. I played as if I had scooped them up and put them in my pocket for luck. As cold as it was, I couldn't bring myself to part with such a sight. I'd be there before I was ready; honestly, I'd probably never be ready. *Here we go,* I thought, trying to organize my emotions into something I could control, even understand.

I had spent time referencing the map, trying to familiarize myself with the huge city. I knew the general location of Kelly's house and had mapped the route from the train tracks. I was fairly confident I would be capable of finding her house.

What adventures were to be had? My anticipation grew, as did the city on the horizon. My mind raced with new life, and I was giddy at the thought of a hot shower.

When finally my eyes were full, I retreated to the wind break between the cars. I organized the bag's contents in preparation for my arrival. I located the mint tin I had found months ago and exhumed its only contents, a half-smoked cigarette. I had been trying to quit for months and lately had been forced to. I had grown bored of looking for discarded remnants, and the novelty had gone. I was saving this one for when I got to Chicago; now that I was almost there, it seemed appropriate. I lit it, and the stale flavor brought me back to Bon, but there was little that didn't remind me of him. Gorgeously dizzy, I sat back to enjoy it and daydream to no particular extent.

Suburban communities began to creep into my limited view. Fences, lots of fences, and debris I couldn't make out in the hazy dark. Not quite sure where the commuting nightmare ended and the actual city began, I watched diligently, enjoying the promise of familiar company. Wrapped in the night, I felt protected and invisible as I made my way to a new adventure.

As the buildings steadily got bigger, I readied myself, strapping the large bag to my back and pulling up my courage. I peered out between the gaps in the train cars, leaning out so I could see where the train was headed. The buildings loomed, still distant. I searched for a soft landing. The ground was powdered with snow, so it was impossible to decipher gravel from sharp basalt. A chance, faith in destiny, I lowered myself to the last rung, took in a breath, and bounded from the train. I landed gracefully enough but worked to steady myself, having gotten so accustomed to constant movement. I took my first steps like a newborn calf but was soon proficient. I followed the tracks till I came to what I thought was the first street on my route and followed it.

The neighborhood intimidated me. It was quiet at one in the morning, but there was some undercurrent of dismal affairs. The small houses and duplexes stood with peeling paint and sun-bleached tricycles in the tracked, snowy lawns. Cars and trucks of every make and model lined the curbs and beaded in the driveways. It felt good to walk, though the harsh, cold wind gusts infiltrated my layers. Guided by the streetlights and disturbed only by the occasional passing car, I progressed steadily.

I realized at around four in the morning that I was hopelessly lost. I had made it this close, and now things began to look so dismal. Having walked for five hours deeper into the Minotaur's maze, I hadn't a clue where I was. None of the street names was even remotely familiar. My body was frozen, and my numb feet kept stumbling over one another. My hands and face burned like fire. My mind was a blurry panic. I fought tears of desperation for fear they would freeze on my cheeks. I didn't know what to do, and my indecision was more disconcerting than being directionless. My eyes search for a place to consult the atlas, but where they fell only filled me with discomfort. I wanted to go home and be safe in the circle of Bon's arms, but he was so far from me now.

If you could collect every tear ever shed in this great city, it would undoubtedly be enough to fill Lake Michigan, should it ever run dry. Unable to prevent aiding in the theoretical salted reserve, my eyes filled. I blinked away the tears that froze before reaching the sidewalk.

So cold. Sweat breaking on my forehead and searching through the bathroom medicine cabinet. Where was she? Far from safe, I feared. A bottle of cold medicine crashed to the counter, along with my stepmother's eyelash curler.

"Bon, are you okay?" A moment later my father's voice rang from the open doorway.

So tired I couldn't speak. My watery eyes tried to focus on him but couldn't. I dizzily leaned against the bathroom counter. "Where is she?" I managed, feeling myself slipping to the floor and then into my fathers' arms.

By dawn, I was all cried out. In the early comforting haze of light, I found a park bench in a small field of snow. I navigated stiffly to sit on the bench, unable to feel the cold of the fresh powder an inch deep on the treated wood. I pulled the atlas from Bon's bag, relishing the soft smell of him lingering in the bag's rough fabric. Studying the atlas lines intently, I tried to get my eyes to comply, but they were swollen, tired, and shaking with the trembling of my shivering body. I determined I was just north of Sixty-Seventh Street, about a mile off track. Crap. Well, at least I knew where I was and had peace of mind knowing that I didn't have to back track.

I dug out the plastic bag of dry cereal, replaced the atlas, and refastened the bag to my shoulders. As I walked I munched on the Lucky Charms knockoff, making quick work of the marshmallows I habitually picked out from among the plainer pieces. Bon use to pick them out for me. Oh, how I missed him.

The sidewalks stretched out into forever. I was sure my pink cowboy boots had caused blisters, but I couldn't feel anything yet. I passed quite an expanse of headstones before reaching my oasis, Kelly's house. It was different than what I had expected: average, two stories with a one-car garage, pale blue with white trim. I hesitated on the shoveled walk leading to the front porch.

Refreshing my courage with the thought of a hot shower, I proceeded. The doorbell seemed to stare me down as I reached a frigged finger toward it. In a moment it was over. I waited for the door to open. I then realized the rude hour in which I had arrived and prayed someone was already awake.

An older woman answered the door in her nightgown, smiling at this dirty stranger.

"Is this Kelly's house?" I shivered.

The woman's bright smile broadened. "You must be a friend of hers." She gestured to invite me into the house.

The rush of warm air could have suffocated me in bliss, and I smiled my thank you.

"She isn't up yet, so I'll go wake her," she gently told me, mounting the stairs beside the front door's linoleum threshold.

I breathed it in, the warmth, and could feel it radiate through me like shockwaves.

As if being rousted from a dream, I found myself in a white bed surrounded by personnel dressed in scrubs with an IV tube protruding from my arm. I scanned for the first set of eyes that could find mine. A nurse, obviously unseasoned by the look of concern across her face, met my gaze and nearly shrieked.

"He's conscious!"

Kelly drearily followed her mother down the stairs, but upon finally deciphering my identity, she was wide awake.

"Echo!" she spouted, moving quickly the last few steps to embrace me. "My god, how did you get here?"

I made eyes in her mother's direction and said nothing.

"You're like a stinky popsicle." She led me upstairs, helping with my bag.

"I had to leave Olympia. Bon went home, and things are kinda a mess right now," I said, trying to recall how much Kelly actually knew.

"Don't worry about it right now. Let's get you warm." She took me to the bathroom, plugged the tub, and adjusted the temperature of the running water. "I'll get you some clothes." She left down the hallway.

I began to peel away the layers: my coat, jacket, long-sleeved button-up flannel, t-shirt, boots, two pairs of socks, and my second pair of pants.

Kelly returned, arms full of fabric. She looked at the pile of clothes on the floor and smirked. "And after all that, you're still dressed."

I stood in jeans and a tank top.

"I'll leave you to it." She smiled, set the new clothes on the counter, and closed the door behind her.

Aw, heaven on earth, I thought, removing my remaining articles of clothing. Mortified at how dirty my skin was, I jumped into the warm water and relaxed my tired muscles. With the extensive collection of liquid soaps and hair products, I pampered myself, feeling vindicated after my ordeal.

Staring at the puckering lines on my hands, I knew I should be dead. I had spent the majority of a month in below freezing temperatures, calling inhospitable rail and highways my residence. Every inch of my body was blotchy red with frostbite, shades of purple like bruises mottled the skin on my toes, yet here I was, a mystery.

I dried and dressed. Kelly had laid out a pair of light-blue jeans, a plain black t-shirt, and a pair of white socks. I had no clean underwear, so I went commando. I gathered up my clothes, washrag, and towel and exited the bathroom. I turned right down the hall then took another right down the stairs. Halfway down, Kelly rounded the banister and looked up at me.

"Hope yer hungry. My mom's making enough pancakes to choke a whale." She waved me to follow, and we walked through the spacious living room beside the kitchen to a small laundry room. Kelly unloaded the bundle in my arms into the washing machine, added detergent, and asked "Do you take softener?"

I shrugged my shoulders, having not the recollection of ever trying it.

She filled the dispenser, placed it, and slammed the washer's lid down. She pulled the knob to start the water then ushered me out.

Kelly led me to the kitchen and fitted me for breakfast. I proceeded to gorge myself stupid. From across the small, round, wooden table, my company tried not to stare, but their eyes always wandered my way. I didn't care; I had been hungry for weeks, trying to conserve provisions. Now I was desperate to make up for all those lost calories. When I had cleared my plate, Kelly's mother smiled and asked if she could get me more. I declined, feeling the walls of my stomach stretching, threatening to squeeze it back up my throat.

"Well, doll," Kelly started, "I've got to go to work in about an hour." She rose from her matching wooden chair and cleared the table. "You could watch TV or go sightseeing, whatever you want to do."

I stood up and followed her into the kitchen. "Actually, I'm exhausted. Would it be cool if I went to sleep?"

She rinsed the dishes. "Of course. You can just crash on my bed."

"My schedule is all fucked up. I've been sleeping during the day, afraid I'd freeze in the night," I said as I helped to load the dishwasher. She said nothing, but her eyes were burning holes in me as they looked for answers.

My eyes would hardly stay open, so Kelly sympathetically led me up to her room.

"I'll be home around three thirty, then we'll drink some beer and bullshit."

I stumbled a little as I crossed her room to the bed. I didn't care that she had a pile of questionable laundry at the foot. I was fed and begging to crash, safe at last.

"That sounds great." I sighed and she gave a giggle before leaving. I immediately submitted to sleep.

"I feel fine!" I told the nurse as she took another blood sample.

"I'm sorry, I know, but we can't seem to figure out what's wrong," she replied in a rehearsed, blank voice.

"Well, that's cuz there is nothing wrong," I said rudely. She shot a glare at me before collecting the tubes of blood and exiting the room.

I had been lying in bed for hours surrounded by puzzled physicians. My father worriedly talked with them and relayed everything they said. Apparently I was suffering from hypothermia with no evident cause. Undoubtedly at my father's whim, the doctors frantically searched for a cause.

My father entered the room, rubbing his hands together. "They want to keep you a few days, just to be sure it doesn't happen again." His eyes were still riddled with guilt, fresh now and timid. He sat down in the chair next to the hospital bed and laid his hands on his thighs. "I'm sorry," he nearly whispered.

"For what?" I was playing naïve. He only looked at me and sighed. Those eyes looked ready to cry; I felt remorseful but wanted to press the apology for an explanation. Damn his stubbornness. An explanation from his lips could prompt my forgiveness. He couldn't confess, I knew. I was a lot like him. I'd hide that which shamed me from even myself. Though I could understand, I needed to know, could he? Did he without doubt betray my love to wolves?

"She can't go home," I said softly. His panicked eyes were afraid to look at me. "They beat her and mentally abused her. When she failed her attempt at suicide, only then did she run from home." I raised my voice, and as he tried to act confused in a halfhearted attempt, I cut him off. "She had a new family in Olympia, people who loved her, who helped show her how worthwhile she really was." I took a breath and shook my head. "She was getting good grades, building a future for herself, and you took it all away." By this time I was nearly yelling at my father, my eyes burning holes on the lids that would not lift to look at me. He kept his eyes to the floor in some introspective deliberation. "If anything bad happens to her, I will never speak to you again."

His eyes lifted from the floor to meet mine with all the shame that came with them. His eyes seemed to plead for forgiveness.

"I just wanted you to stay home." He sighed. "You kept talking about leaving again, to go be with her. I thought that if she went home, maybe you would wait till you were both grownup." He nearly sobbed. "I'm sorry, I never thought she would elude the police. The both of you should be safe at home, growing up like normal kids."

"We aren't normal kids," I replied with dry resentment. I reflected on my own words, seeing the train whistle winds tangling her hair while I bathed her in smiles. The way the setting sun made her skin look orange and electric, radiantly soft. My heart throbbed thinking of her, my love for her making me love the world that betrayed us. Through her, it seemed possible to forgive my misguided father, but only for her.

"Help me find her, and all will be forgiven," I said, reaching a hand to rest on his knee. He nodded, fearful to speak and have his words come out in sobs.

I stayed in the hospital for a few days. I had more visitors than I expected. Virgil, a starry-eyed gay boy from school, stopped by to bring my missed schoolwork. I wasn't his type, but we were friends. I could tell it made my father uncomfortable. Virgil and I made plans to see a movie when I got out.

When my father came to check me out of the hospital, he brought with him my soul's morphine, a letter from Echo. He handed it to me with a shamed, sorrowful smile. Her letter promised that all would be better soon, and I believed. In the middle of the hospital hallway, I slid down the wall to sit on the floor reading those words hungrily yet thoroughly. At the precious words "I love you," I could feel my blood warm and disperse endorphins to kiss any minor discomfort away. She promised to write again when she was eighteen, but inside I knew for fact I wouldn't have to wait that long. I would find her. Within her letter she rested her fears and hopes, and sent her love. My little girl was all on her own, and I was on the hospital floor soaking up her recent last words. Unable to care for the wondering eyes that looked on me, I lifted the letter to my nose and inhaled. There she was. I closed my eyes and held the letter to my heart, unwilling, for now, to exhale and rejoin my existence. It lasted only long enough for me to wish it lasted longer. I opened my eyes. My father stood smiling at me in slight embarrassment.

"Is she all right?" he asked, genuinely concerned.

"She was when she wrote the letter," I said as I stood up, "though a bit lost and lonely."

"You're really in love with her, aren't you?" It had finally dawned on him.

"She's my Juliet, my Cleopatra, my everything," I answered, joining him to make our exit. "I would do anything for her." He gave me a wise smile that set me in vague confusion.

When we got to my father's car, he asked me, "Have the two of you had sex yet?"

I really didn't want to have this talk, but there it was. I was hot with embarrassment.

"No," I responded simply.

He appeared shocked. "I thought you two spent a few years together."

"Yeah, but we were always too busy making love to have sex." I relished his confusion, perfectly aware of my play with words.

"You haven't had intercourse?" he had to reiterate, and I couldn't help laughing.

"Noooo, conversations and kisses, cuddling and holding hands." I buckled my seatbelt, and he started the engine. "We are content to make collages instead of babies."

With that he gave an "aw." He finally got it. "I know you think she's the only girl for you, but there are a lot of wonderful girls out there."

"Don't," I interrupted. "You don't know her. I've never met anyone who could look at their own suffering and sing to spite it. She knows just what to say, what to do, to fix me when I fall apart. I feel whole when I'm with her, and I wouldn't want to imagine my life without her."

He gave a reluctant nod and smile, nearly dropping his forced topic. "Just keep in mind that that kind of love seems to end in tragedy, the kind that wrecks you forever." Not another word, just the tear in his eye that never fell.

I felt a lot of resentment. Echo and I were quite aware of the odds we were facing. I didn't need my father to point it out. She and I were both from broken homes; did that make us broken people? We didn't dwell to think so. I didn't remember my mother; she left when I was a toddler—or was driven out, I didn't know. I'd always been close to my grandmother; her caring hands were the closest thing I had to a mother while my father spent years dating. My grandmother had been widowed nearly twenty years ago and never bothered to love again. She looked like my mother would have. When I was ten, we got news my mother had died in a car crash. She had my name tattooed over her heart; I saw it at the funeral. Because they failed and my father finds my stepmother's company lacking, did that mean Echo and I will fall from love too? The way I saw it now, there was no way we would ever be crestfallen. Words of wisdom, and I scoffed to myself.

Life returned to a more normal stagnation. Virgil and I went to the movies, started taking lunch together in the alley. We would bum change and engage random people in lewd interviews. We asked rhetorical questions and made them feel stupid. We were simply finding distractions till graduation.

My father ran computer searches for Echo on the Internet that yielded no results. Her letter was postmarked in South Dakota, but I knew she wouldn't still be there. My father contacted the South Dakota police looking for Echo or even a Jane Doe, with no results. I appreciated the effort, but I knew where she was. I just wasn't so sure if I should let him know. If Echo was going through South Dakota, she was crossing the country to see Kelly. I just hoped she would stay there a few more months. I didn't know where Kelly lived, save for the city, but I knew I would find Echo. I could hardly believe my little baby had crossed the northern states in late winter, but I could feel inside she was safe now. It explained my bout with hypothermia, though, and it tickled me to think we were so connected. I tried to share my thoughts on the matter with my father. He told me it was merely coincidence, but I knew better.

Chapter 16

I quickly fell in love with Chicago; it went on for days, leaving me with the impression of endless possibilities. I spent the majority of the daylight hours taking in the sights and pigging out on hot dogs. The city was expensive, so I amused myself with free things like riding the elevators in some of the skyscrapers and hanging out on the lakefront. I went to the Museum of Science and Industry. It had free admission on Thursday, and I would walk around till they closed, never tiring of the extensive exhibits.

Kelly let me use her ten-speed bike with an open invitation. More of the city opened up to me as I was now more mobile—the lakefront, Oakwood Cemetery, and beneath the tall buildings.

I felt determined to learn the city front to back. That way when love found its way back to me, I could show him my city. I missed Bon terribly. I took pictures with an old 35-mm camera I found in Kelly's garage. I hoped that someday soon I would be able to share them with him. I yearned and prepared for that day, wondering when it would come. Would he come find me after his birthday, or after graduation, or would he wait till I contacted him after my eighteenth? Who knew. The uncertainty caused me a lot of stress.

On Kelly's days off, we took the buses and subways around the city, and she would show me her favorite places: a coffee shop and bookstore, a second-hand clothing boutique, and Tower Records, where she worked. She paid my admission and took me to the Adler Planetarium and Astronomy Museum. It was amazing. She told me of a few other places that had free admission on certain days, and I planned to go some other time.

Often I went with Kelly to her band practice, and she let me borrow a purple Fender and portable pig-nosed amp for panhandling. She took me to the local punk shows and keg parties, and we forged a watertight friendship. There was so much to do, so many things to see, but there was always something missing—a smile and a soft hand to hold. I think the more fun I had, the more I missed and wished I could share it with him.

I needed to find a job. Kelly and her mother had no hang-ups about supporting me, but I felt useless anyway. Vicky, Kelly's mother, was a children's short story author and made plenty of money, but I only felt like a leech in the horn of plenty. Panhandling in Chicago was good, but not steady. I wanted to save money for when Bon got here; I wanted to take him to all the galleries and museums. I daydreamed about getting a legitimate apartment, maybe going to college, and I blushed at the idea of someday starting a family. I needed a good job, but without a Social Security card or birth certificate, it seemed impossible, not to mention the risk of being exposed.

One morning over breakfast, Vicky had a novel idea.

"Kelly, why don't you just let Echo borrow your identity till she's eighteen?" She spoke almost too casually.

"What do you mean?" Kelly inquired, her mouth still full of scrambled egg.

"I'll take her down to the DMV with your birth certificate and Social Security number, and I'll say she's you. We'll get her an ID card, and she can get a job."

I kept my mouth closed, hoping Kelly would go for it. Not only could I get a job, but I could also buy tobacco and lottery tickets.

"Do you think that will work?" Kelly grinned deviously.

"I don't see why not."

Kelly laughed and gave the perfect answer. "Okay, worth a try."

I thanked Kelly and her mother a thousand times over. That afternoon, Vicky and I went down to the DMV. The plan went off without a hitch. I had an identification card that stated I was nineteen and named Kelly Newel. I treasured the plastic card and felt a new life waiting for me.

The next morning I started putting in applications, avoiding the fast food industry. When the day started, I was scared that someone would know I was lying, but somewhere after the third application, I felt more confident. I stumbled across a staffing company and elected to try out my new identity.

The office was quiet, like a library. I walked to the closest desk. The nameplate read Becky, and I said "hello" as small as I felt. She looked up from the stack of papers she was mulling over and smiled.

"You looking to apply to anywhere specific?" she inquired, halfway returning to her papers.

"No, just anywhere," I replied.

Becky opened the drawer in her desk, got out an application, and fixed it to a clipboard that had a pen attached with a white length of string.

"Fill this out and bring it back to me." She gently smiled while handing over the clipboard.

Within an hour and a half, I had taken a quiz on how to use a tape measure, submitted a urine sample for analysis, and had a date to start work on Monday. The job was labor in a factory, doing what I didn't know yet. I was scared and had only three days to find my courage, along with steel-toed boots.

I took my time getting home, sorting my thoughts. I was excited and proud, but at the same time I was terrified. I was only sixteen and a half and going to work in a factory. It was certainly not my dream job, but it paid better money than I had ever had before.

I took Kelly's bike to work. It took thirty minutes to get there, and I was five minutes early. I was placed in packaging along with another girl much older than me. Sarah was talkative and loud, so it balanced out my shyness. We were taught to put stickers sporting the company logo on the large pieces of equipment. Conveyer belts, to be exact. Later we were taught to lift them with a two-ton-capacity crane and put them into wooden crates, drill holes, and bolt them in. By the end of the day, I was exhausted. By the end of the week, I was rich, or at least I saw it that way.

I treated my hosts to dinner at a Greek restaurant and learned that I don't like Greek olives but I love gyros. I got myself new work clothes, pocketing fifty and putting the rest in a tape case for saving. After a few weeks of my new forty-hour-a-week job, I grew to find things in life painfully routine.

I had earned my driver's license and now looked for a suitable used vehicle. I had around $3,500, but I was hoping not to spend so much. The more of my savings I spent on a car, the longer I had to wait before I could afford to find Echo.

I had a mind to take Virgil with me, but I could just imagine Echo's reaction when I rolled up with a pretty gay boy. We had become good friends, to my slander at school, but I didn't care. I'd graduate soon enough and never see the majority of them again. Strangely, I was a little frightened to go find her alone. I kept my plans to myself, so as not to alert my father's anxiety. I didn't want to have to justify my love. I was just going to leave when I had enough capital for food and gas. I'd find her. Whenever I thought about it, I got butterflies and felt as though I was doing something more important than life itself. After my father's betrayal, I no longer cared if I had his blessing. Once it was legal, I was leaving.

My father and I went to several different car dealerships, but I was very specific on the vehicle's qualifications. My car had to be decent on gas, white like the fabled steed, and within my price range. About the time my father became disinterested in helping me, I found it: a little white truck owned by an elderly couple in Virgil's neighborhood. They were asking $3,500, but I managed to talk them down to three grand even. After registering it and getting plates, I was broke. I'd have to save all summer. This fact bummed me out, but it was a very nice truck, which consoled me.

Echo would love it; the truck was shiny, with fair upholstery, air conditioning, and a tape player. I could hardly stand the wait. She would be walking down the street or exiting a building or house and see me. Just like that, genuine surprise, and as always thrilled to see me. She would climb in, and we would drive into the sunset and find the "happily ever after" Disney promised us.

Graduation day came, and I was disappointed that I wasn't more excited. I was pleased to have accomplished my diploma and to be that much closer to heading out on my next adventure. The thrill of so much never came. This miniscule achievement could never compare to outrunning the police, earning a decent wage by panhandling, or discovering she loved me back. Things just weren't quite comparable to the life I used to know.

My father threw a party in my honor, and I was given much praise by family and friends. My grandmother had made my cake and came to inquire about my future plans. I had to insist she not tell, and then told her I planned to find Echo in Chicago. Her eyes sparkled with reminiscent adventures in love. She made a gift of five hundred dollars, telling me in her aging, gentle voice to "find her and never forget why you went looking."

By the party's early conclusion, I had over a thousand dollars to put toward the future. More than all the money in the world, I had my grandmother's blessing and encouragement.

I worked as much as I could, pulling double shifts and getting overtime. I stashed all the money I made in a coffee tin hidden beneath the clutter in my closet. By Echo's birthday, I had $2,764. It would probably be enough, but it didn't feel right yet, or maybe I was just scared. At the birth of August, I could feel it was time. I had another grand saved, and the constellations were right.

I took pains to write my father a letter that encompassed my actions. I packed up my things and disappeared in the middle of the night. I lost myself in the space between the lines in the road, experiencing a progression of every emotion, but for the most part I was ecstatic. I kept the tape deck rolling as I sped my way across the country, sleeping at rest stops in my truck and eating only when I stopped for gas. The anticipation of her surprised smile kept me going on little more than four hours of sleep every night.

My eyes swept the faces of everyone I saw, searching for things familiar. Her hair, eyebrows, her walk, sometimes I thought I could smell her on the breeze, but I was tirelessly searching for those eyes. The closer I came to Chicago, the more things reminded me of her.

Nothing ever comes so easily. Somewhere in Iowa, my alternator went out. Sitting with my chin resting on my palms on a bench outside of a quaint mechanic's shop, I wondered at my current predicament. How could this have happened? Was I too hasty in my departure? For whatever reason, I was going to be stuck here for a week or more. The mechanic had told me he would have to order the new alternator; business was blissfully busy for him. A week! A week. But I was so close, she was so close. As I sat there dissolving in my self-pity, I had a realization. I felt stupid for not coming to the obvious sooner. Had I become so pampered? I could just hitchhike to Chicago. So what if I couldn't have my white steed? I could have her. We could come back for the truck; after all, it was a mere possession.

I got up from the bench and went inside the garage where my mechanic Carl was working under a sedan's hood. I gave him the truck keys and told him I'd see him in a week. I pulled from my truck what I could carry and headed for the highway.

The job didn't mean all that much to me, so why was I so upset? I got laid off, along with the other temps, so why was I taking it so personally? I did a good job, and I was never late. I cried a little riding Kelly's bike home. I didn't want to tell Kelly and Vicky; I was ashamed. I felt terrible and wanted to crawl into a hole and hide. *Maybe that's what I'll do,* I thought, wiping away the tears in my eyes. All summer I'd wanted to hop a train or stick out my thumb, and now fall was fast approaching. I had stayed, content to wait for Bon, but now I felt as though I had to run from my shame. *Just a little while. Maybe I'll take a week or two in Maine.* I'd never been to Maine before. I wanted to get drunk; I wanted to forget my rejection. I knew what to expect when I got home. Kelly and her mother would take turns giving me "chin up" clichés, then Kelly would get me drunk and convince me to stay.

Where was Bon? Was he coming? In my current frame of mind, I figured he had found someone new, and they were preparing to go to the same university, and the next time I would see him, he would be married with a few kids, and our meeting would be accidental. I thought my way into despair.

Progress was slower than I had hoped. It seemed no one was too keen on picking up a hitchhiker. I hadn't thought to pick up

161

another atlas bearing railroad routes, and the ones I found for purchase where useless. The train tracks I found ran north to south, and I needed to go east by northeast. Disheartened, I sat by the tracks hoping for a north-bound train, negatively wondering how far it might take me in the wrong direction.

The sun set, and I was left in the dark with nothing but my loneliness. It seemed as though the whole world was against me. The full moon shed its light so that I could not hide, even from myself. The breeze only whispered, and not to me. How could I have been so foolish to think I could find her in a metropolis? People who were born there may never meet. It's only a fool who puts so much faith in chance. Apparently, I was just that. I decided then that I would take that leap of stupidity. Due to lack of options, I would take the next train that came my way. If the train headed south, I would return to my truck and go back to Arizona to wait for the day Echo divulged her location. If the train headed north, I would try to find Echo in Chicago. So now with my mind made up, I had to wait in the dark.

After hours of detesting my own company, boredom tucked me into my dreams. With my head resting on my bag, I lay in the brush, stolen from myself.

I had cashed my last pay check, locked up Kelly's bike at a park, and was speeding away from my shame. The night was the same shade as me, blue. Bon didn't come after his eighteenth birthday, or after his graduation. Still, like a fool, I had waited. I was a bit too old for fairy tales.

I didn't care where I was going, only that I had left everything behind me.

Sometime in the night, I woke to my destiny's train whistle. Uncertain as to the direction of its origin, I readied myself. My heart sank as I realized it was a train heading south. I would be going home.

I hid from the headlight and was choosy in picking a car. A gray tanker would do nicely. Like a hundred times before, I grabbed hold of the ladder and tried to ascend, but some article of clothing was caught on something I couldn't make out in the dark. As I tried to free myself with one hand, almost in slow motion, my secure foot slipped. Dangling, my panic induced me to perspire, compromising my grip. I was going to die. I supposed love had no more use for me. I reached up with my loose hand, desperately searching in the dark for anything to grab onto. I wondered if my demise would be painful. I hoped Echo would understand, and I said good-bye for the first and last time. As my last finger slipped, two hands reached for me, grabbing hold of my backpack's shoulder straps. With help, I scrambled to the grated platform. There in my arms was the sum of all god's secrets smiling back at me.

As if by a will far greater than my own embodied by a universal script, I had saved him without the strength or consciousness to do so. Like a dream, there he was, safe in my arms. We wouldn't let

163

go, not ever, and always wondering when we would wake up. I had taken what I thought was my train to nowhere, but it turned out to be the only one I would ever need again. Oh destiny, how I fawn on you.

As the train whistle blew, time stood still, and two children found their place in this crazy world. Hand in hand, the world will bend to the soft whims of lovers. Listen and believe because love speaks in sighs. If the wind is blowing too hard, listen closer.